HERR NIGHTINGALE
and the SATIN WOMAN

WILLIAM KOTZWINKLE
Illustrated by
JOE SERVELLO

ALFRED A. KNOPF   NEW YORK   1978

THIS IS A BORZOI BOOK
PUBLISHED BY ALFRED A. KNOPF, INC.

Copyright © 1978 by William Kotzwinkle and Joe Servello
All rights reserved under International and Pan-American Copyright Conventions. Published in the United States by Alfred A. Knopf, Inc., New York, and simultaneously in Canada by Random House of Canada Limited, Toronto. Distributed by Random House, Inc., New York.

Library of Congress Cataloging in Publication Data
Kotzwinkle, William.
Herr Nightingale and the satin woman.
I. Title.
PZ4.K872Hg 1978 [PS3561.085]   813'.5'4   78-54911
ISBN 0-394-50106-3

Manufactured in the United States of America
First Edition

A Note on the Type

The text of this book was set in film in Korinna, a typeface originated in 1904 at H. Berthold AG in Berlin. International Typeface Corporation of New York introduced the present-day Korinna, and the roman letterforms appeared in 1974. They were the work of Ed Benguiat, Victor Caruso, and the staff of Photo-Lettering, Inc. In 1977, the italic of Korinna drawn by Ed Benguiat appeared.

Combining strongly antithetic traits, Korinna has met with overwhelming contemporary approval.

The book was composed by Haber Typographers, New York, New York. It was printed by Halliday Lithographers, West Hanover, Massachusetts, and bound by Sendor Bindery, New York, New York.
Design by Kathleen Westray and Margaret Wagner.

I know that he seeks me, even now, and regret every encounter that tempted me to reveal some part of myself. Inevitably what others perceived in such moments was not me—how could it be?—but it sufficed to create an identity which could be traced.

My vanity, my need to share, has given him the thread. Over and over again I play out these encounters. I've realized it could not be otherwise. In the inner circle of our profession, there are those of whom it can be said—no one knows they are on this earth.

"Then you've dealt with Nightingale?" asks Inspector Bagg.

"Naturally," answers the Mole. "But this was in Cairo."

Bagg smiles. "It was you who financed the uprising?"

"Of course," says the Mole.

"Then you know this associate of Nightingale, the one they call the Satin Woman?"

"She was an agent of Baron Oppenheim. Very young and very beautiful," says the Mole, with something like a sigh.

The Satin Woman with Nightingale, along the Rhine at twilight; he speaks of business for a long time, whom they must see, how they'll be cheated. Gradually, as the castles on the rolling hills are lit, his voice grows quieter, less suspicious of the world. Unseen figures move through the distant castle rooms, turning them into stone lanterns that shine down to the water, and she sees the lamps affect him, feels a mist embrace her, a smuggler's soul moving shyly. He begins to reminisce, about the war in Egypt, the force called *Pasha I,* and men claimed by the wind. She listens, moved by the thread of sadness in his memory, for Herr Nightingale is supposed to care for nothing but money and good cigars.

She's cautious of responding to his tenderness, for she loves him enough as it is, which is to say—she is still able to leave him.

"These fragments," he says, staring out the window. "I've often sought for some way to bring them together. I mean the faces. An officer standing with a thin cane in his hand. We were moving out from Beersheba. Was he killed? I don't know who he was. There are others, stamped in my brain for no reason."

The Rhine has darkened, is only reflections now, on a black ribbon. "Curious, isn't it?" he asks, looking away from the window, and toward her. "These chance pieces of time."

Avoiding his eyes, she takes out her mirror, touches at her hair.

"I find it curious," says Nightingale, returning his gaze to the shimmering lanterns.

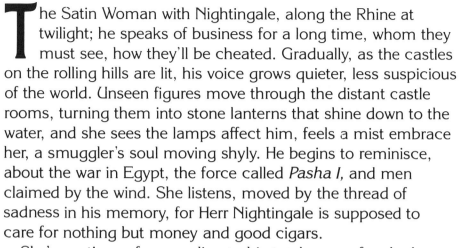

Inspector Bagg, in Berlin, finds the Nachtigall family—an old man with a card shop, a doting wife, a cat by the stove. Their mantelpiece betrays them with its picture, of a soldier, the youthful Nightingale. Bagg is almost sorry to see it there, for his own father kept a shop in Lancashire, a little shop like this, where little was ever sold.

He purchases a postcard; while paying for it steps closer to the mantelpiece and smiles, inquiring about the decorations on the young soldier's chest. Both parents speak at once, about the 60th Artillery Battalion.

"…in Egypt. The battle of Suez, of Romani, of Gaza, under Von Kressenstein. In 1917, wounded…" The mother points to the medal.

"An importer now," says the father, with a gesture to indicate his son has gone far beyond the four walls of the little shop, and the confines of the simple frame on the mantelpiece. "He travels…"

Bagg nods, smiles again and, slipping the card into his pocket, goes slowly toward the door, looking at some sealing wax, some stationery. The door surprises him, he fumbles with the latch, clumsily bids them good day, casting a fog around himself, through which he knows they cannot see the man who hunts their son, Lieutenant Nachtigall of the 60th Artillery.

Nachtigall on the Lake of Dreams, with the Satin Woman: He's persuaded to take a shipment to the Far East, to the gates of the Forbidden City.

"It will travel as perfume," explains their host. "Shall we say attar of roses? At all events, the contents will be the Dream. Your contact is the art dealer, Chang of Moon Pagoda Street. He has, I believe, some machine guns to sell. You must make your own arrangements on that."

The yacht rocks lightly, water lapping at its bow; yellow deck lanterns, wicks turned low, click softly back and forth, as dreams move on the lake, attracted by the light, but dissolving as they near it, only to reappear again beyond its glow. They are exotics, with crystalline forms, into which the Satin Woman is drawn, despite the gentle warnings of the host.

"It takes, I believe, four-thousand pounds of blossoms to make a pound of rose oil, but the blossoms in a single dream are too numerous to weigh or count. They'll capture your soul, my dear, if you're not careful."

"I'm familiar with dreams."

"Of the ordinary sort, but these—" He points at the moving waters with his glass. "—these are quintessential creations. I wouldn't treat them carelessly."

"Yet you bottle them…"

"At great cost. That is why—" He smiles at Nightingale. "—they are so expensive."

"And illegal," adds Nightingale, returning the smile.

"Yes, of course," says the host, inserting his monocle and letting his gaze fall on the Satin Woman once more. "One can't have dreams like these running around the streets of Europe. Really—" He stares at her with his good eye. "—they're only fit for a Chinaman. Don't you agree, Nightingale?"

Nightingale sights over the edge of his glass as a dream dances nearer, its crystal fan expanding like a thousand-fingered hand, gesturing seductively, with increasing familiarity, with an intimacy that suddenly grips innumerable facets of his nature and reflects them in a tessellated surface that is unbearable, because unthinkable. He puts down his glass and looks away.

"I suggest we go below," says the host. "The damned things are worse than mosquitoes."

The Satin Woman lingers on the steps to the galley, as the host and Nightingale talk below, of the customs arrangements required to slip the attar of dreams into China.

Bagg poles along the Lake of Dreams, too late. The sun has risen, the yacht is gone, as are the dreams. It's no surprise; chasing Nightingale has become a way of life, and always the smuggler is one step ahead, fading into the mist. Bagg accepts the defeat, as usual, confident that he's closing on Nightingale by slow degrees. He steps onto shore, abandoning the boat he'd found, unaware that it is a lingering dream, and that he's actually been walking on water.

Had he known, he would've collared the dream and run it in; formerly of the Thames Division of the Yard, he's used to dealing with depraved water spirits, who'd leave a navvy's pick-ax in your skull for the fun of it.

But the trail leads outward from the lake, to the North Sea, and he follows it, intent on one thing only—Nightingale's arrest. Informers, getting wind of a heavy and closely guarded shipment, advance him on his way, through towns and villages where the Dream has passed, and passing wrecked the sleep of its inhabitants, fantastic succubi leaking from a broken bottle of the attar, luring young men to the highways and old men to the stars.

Wherever he stops, Bagg gives assurances to the local authorities that Scotland Yard is on the job, and closing fast.

Nightingale prepares for the journey: The shipment is asleep in the hold of the steamer *Kongmoon.* The Satin Woman reclines on her couch in their waterfront hotel. Nightingale studies his old, much-repaired map of China; the familiar creases, the dog-eared edges, bring memories, and expectation. He lays his pistol upon the Forbidden City, looks at the Satin Woman.

"You have no wish to go?"

"No," she answers, from a different dimension, an open bottle of dreams on the table beside her. If she goes, she well knows, she'll become addicted to attar of roses.

"What will you do?" asks Nightingale.

"Please, darling, I'm not thinking quite clearly at the moment."

Nightingale puts away his pistol, folds the map. "We'll meet in Cairo. If there are machine guns to be had, I can get rid of them easily there."

"Whatever you like," she answers, drifting where images gather and merge, always into a central form, the hulking shadow of the English detective who moves toward her now, clad in mist, limping slightly, pursuing her even in reverie, with his face of a bulldog, his ridiculous shoes, and the smell of ginger about him.

She turns on the couch, away from the apparition, which floats by the lamp and then vanishes. To be free of the spectre she has only to desert Nightingale.

She toys with her beads, seeing different men there, among them some who might still be hers, their figures curving on the beads, and moving, toward curving little houses, with gardens where the guests do not arrive furtively, nor carry smuggled ammunition and black-market currency.

"If you'd dispose of the detective," she says, covering the bead bearing a bulldog face.

"He's a man of some experience. He moves with caution." Nightingale pours out a drink, settles back in his chair, confident of eliminating their Inspector Bagg, but one can't make the moment; it makes itself.

The last dream vapor curls from the bottle, toward him, taking the shape not of Bagg, but of the unknown officer some twenty years gone, profiled in the sun, an Iron Cross of the first class over his heart, its silver edges gleaming. Slowly he turns toward Nightingale, but looks on past him, and the passage of cavalry envelops the scene.

The Satin Woman stands, goes to the window. The street is empty, but she hears a scuffling sound, of a man who limps, somewhere in the fog.

Nightingale is beside her then, rough blunt fingers tracing the line of beads at her throat. The window's closed; she's imagined footsteps. And the other faces in the beads, the men of respectable position, are gone. Herr Nightingale puts them quite out of the question, with his smuggler's hands, running riches down the length of her, through the torn nets, the seaweed, the mimosa along the shore.

Bagg sits, bathing his foot in ginger. The fragments inside his ankle, from a homemade bomb thrown by a mad Russian in Victoria Station, have never come out properly. Since that time, wild-eyed men with disordered beards make him nervous, and not a few innocent inventors and good-natured zanies have been collared by him in public places.

He adds more hot water and watches his foot get red. It's a lonely life; his heart flies out, to a dear little widow on Minver Place in Bermondsey, adept in the preparation of shepherd's pie and, thinks Bagg, a good hand at the ginger bath too, though her son is frequently arrested for bustle-punching in the underground. An eager lad; likes to feel a tender bottom. Well, don't we all, on occasion.

And here I sit far from home, where dear little widows aren't easily met.

He stirs his foot around, exciting the circulation.

Flo's a find, no mistake about it. But if her son is collared again while I'm gone, some other detective's liable to have shepherd's pie. And the ginger bath too. With little Flo stepping forth in her curlers and towel.

They walk along the waterfront, past import shops displaying island masks, crude nets and pottery. The Satin Woman stops, Nightingale beside her, handling a garish Hindu sword, idly, as one handles a memory; Captain Agah had one like it, he recalls, and the jewels flashed as Agah waved it in the desert at the French and British aeroplanes, defying them to drop a bomb on him personally.

Chance pieces, the fragments of time.

"Yes please, may I help you." The owner of the shop comes from the back room, unwrapping his chin. "Earrings of that quality can no longer be gotten from Bombay, madame, I have spoken the truth. Yes please, try them on."

The Satin Woman takes the earrings, wanders deeper into the shop. "What is in that cage?"

"Personal pet, madame, a cricket, not for sale at any price."

"May I see him?"

"Of course please."

The cage is lowered, and the Satin Woman peeks in the tiny windows. The cricket is dining, but upon seeing her immediately rises. A strange signal passes through her nerves, and she draws back, shocked by the delicate sensation that only gradually subsides, as the owner praises the handiwork of the cage, as well as the cricket's character.

"How much?" asks Nightingale.

"Impossible, dear sir, I cannot sell the little friend who is my good luck and helps me with the crossword puzzle."

"Fifty kroner."

"The cage alone is worth that much, if I may say so. Here, ladies and gentleman, observe the carpeting and the newly installed wall panel."

Nightingale and the owner haggle over price, while the Satin Woman browses, aware of the cricket's eyes still on her.

They share a midnight supper in their room. The cricket plays his piano softly. Nightingale has no wish to leave her, feels the parting already.

"What is that he's playing?" asks the Satin Woman.

"Satie," says Nightingale, pouring the wine.

The gentle, haunting theme is repeated. The windows of the cage cast rosettes of yellow light on the table; the flame of a tiny candelabra burns within.

Nightingale studies the Satin Woman's face in the flickering glow. She moves her arm, and the sleeve of her dressing gown falls forward, in such a way he feels it in himself, feels a feminine fabric fall and move deep within him, and disappear as suddenly, hinting of the world that could be his were he to surrender all.

And the music of the cricket seems to tell him how, to give up pride and folly.

But he sails at dawn, away from her, with a fortune in dreams.

"Come with me," he asks.

"No," she answers. Pride and folly aren't his alone. And the cricket plays, still more softly as the candles grow dim.

ightingale sails: Like fireflies in a jar, the dreams shine within their bottles and light seeps from the crates, enchanting the hold.

Inspector Bagg on a sister ship, the *Kowloon,* attempts to kindle a romance with a portly woman bound for Hong Kong. Her nervous little dog bites him on the bad ankle, and he tips his hat.

The Satin Woman motors inland, the cricket cage on the seat beside her. The cricket entertains her with popular tunes, which she harmonizes—a façade, of course, this light conversation and song; both realize something deeper awaits them.

She has her favorite inns, hidden in the forests of Austria, and she walks the secluded autumnal paths, the cricket riding on her collar. Her perfume takes him over; she has dabbed it on her throat, perhaps, or just behind her ear. A song of courtship escapes him momentarily, before he comes to his senses.

Another couple from the inn appears on the path. The Satin Woman stops, they speak. They think her quite alone; if they see the cricket, he appears as nothing more than a lifelike pin. The Satin Woman is amused, then startled, for their pleasantries grow faint behind the voice of the cricket, which she hears inside her forehead, faintly tingling, electric. Yet he is motionless on her collar, except for his thin feelers, which slowly search the air.

"What is it?" she asks him, in silence, even as she continues conversation with the guests of the inn.

"The sorrow the wind has gathered," he answers, and she sees the wind has passed them on the path, and feels the intimacy of its touch, as on fine quivering antennae threaded from her hair.

The guests continue speaking: "And are you stopping long?"

"No," she says, falling into step with them. "I leave tomorrow."

"A pity. The harvest festival is next week. There will be dancing…"

The wind turns swiftly back, wearing a cape of dead leaves and sash of white fireweed, and passes again. Dark sensory structures rise from her brow to gather the whirling wisdom, and she sways with it, partner to its stately saraband.

At the doorway of the inn, she regains herself, quieting the gift the wind and the cricket have given her, so she can proceed to the dinner table and share in the discussion of politics and autumn foliage.

They motor on, through Paris, to Saint-Cloud. In the shadow of the Grand Cascade he struggles against the song of courtship once more, for he has no wish to be involved. He has his cage, his library, his meditations. She climbs the long Allée du Château, through the deserted park, the cage swinging on her finger. The bare trees and fading flowers release secrets which play in her hair and over her skin. From the high hill, Paris is visible—Montmartre, the Arc de l'Etoile, the Eiffel Tower, and she herself is a tower. The signals she receives are faint, but reassuring.

"Let me out now," says the cricket.

She opens the cage, watches him hop away, knowing he can easily vanish in the grass.

He proceeds into the leaves, along the pulse of the earth, letting it pop him into the air and float him down again. The surges are powerful and his road is clear, into the lavender and thyme—but he returns. For the comfort and protection of his cage, he tells himself.

Yet he knows differently. She stands on the hillside, a wreath of signals in her hair, elegant as a praying mantis, and just as dangerous.

Suddenly the song of courtship bursts from him, full-blown, impossible to contain any longer. He commands the hillside, shattering the tranquillity of the statues. Chirping and whirling at her feet, he flings the tune wildly, feels it ignite the town of Saint-Cloud and pass along the railway to Paris, where it must, he is certain, inflame the boulevards. It is out of season, still it can't be helped. Men, women, and cockroaches will be shifting nervously at the cafés. The dying grass will resurrect, certain wines will mysteriously blow their corks.

This is the grand madrigal of the cricket, I will not be stopped. The female can't resist the song of the stridulating male.

"Such a pretty song," she says, as he falls exhausted. "Does it easily translate?"

"It concerns itself with prodigious leaping," he answers, and slinks back into his cage.

Nightingale at the gates of the Forbidden City: The attar of roses is received by Art Dealer Chang of Moon Pagoda Street. They dine at the back of his shop, in the garden. Beyond its walls peddlers pass, playing their whistles and horns. The shipment is opened, and sampled.

"Genuine," says Art Dealer Chang, the vapor swelling his brain. He breathes deeply, dream attar mingled with pomegranate and pine blowing down from the forests of the Imperial Residence. With this, thinks Chang, raising the cut-glass bottle, I will gain access to the Throne Hall of Supreme Harmony.

Desiring a single taste of it, the clerks and undersecretaries will invite me to stroll with them by the Pearl Concubine's Well.

"Garlic," cry the peddlers. *"Rice cake and noodles."*

In time I'll be laughing with the Chairman of the Great Board of Works, a new munitions contract in my sleeve; possibly something might open in silk and dye-stuffs as well, or in the selling of posthumous honors.

All blessings will converge, thanks to Herr Nightingale, whose prices are, however, too high. But a well-placed bullet in the back of his head will remove that one obstacle to my ascent on the Staircase of Flowering Virtue.

"Machine guns? Yes, of course. Your servant, Chang of Moon Pagoda Street, will arrange all."

"Ginseng. Needles. Lucky-day Almanac…"

Le Havre: The Satin Woman sleeps. The cricket has retired to his cage, is reading by the fire. Quite unexpectedly, the cage lifts itself from the dresser and circles the room.

He leaps from his chair; he'd been warned about Indian-made cages, that their mystical yearnings would finally arise, but he hadn't expected levitation, not from solid brass.

Too late now, the cage is floating out the open window. He topples backward, the carpet sliding underneath him. Below is the city, above the night sky. He peers through the porthole and catches his breath. The cage is accelerating, toward the stars.

Bagg makes friends with the Pekinese too late. The *Kowloon* docks in an hour.

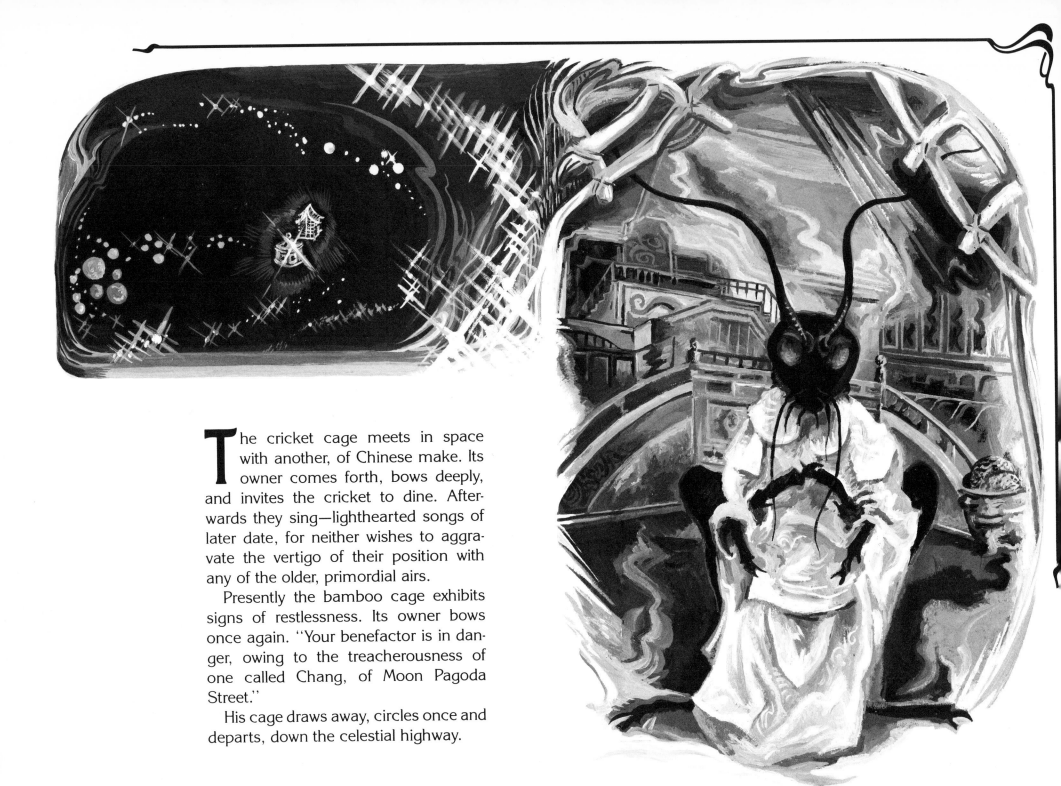

The cricket cage meets in space with another, of Chinese make. Its owner comes forth, bows deeply, and invites the cricket to dine. Afterwards they sing—lighthearted songs of later date, for neither wishes to aggravate the vertigo of their position with any of the older, primordial airs.

Presently the bamboo cage exhibits signs of restlessness. Its owner bows once again. "Your benefactor is in danger, owing to the treacherousness of one called Chang, of Moon Pagoda Street."

His cage draws away, circles once and departs, down the celestial highway.

Nightingale starts from sleep, pistol drawn, goes to the door, opens it upon an empty hallway.

He adjusts the window, prowls the room nervously, anxiety playing along his brow, so that he wipes it again and again, as if to brush away a gathering web.

But it keeps descending, fine and tingling, until he listens, head tipped backward, to what it has to say.

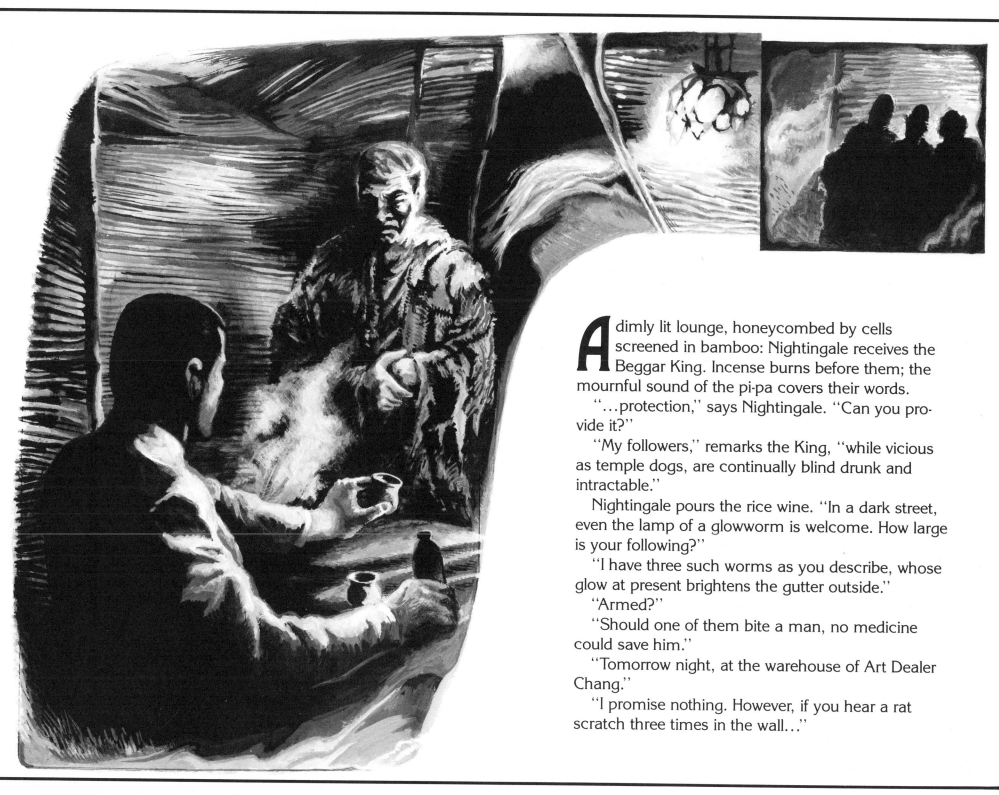

A dimly lit lounge, honeycombed by cells screened in bamboo: Nightingale receives the Beggar King. Incense burns before them; the mournful sound of the pi-pa covers their words.

"...protection," says Nightingale. "Can you provide it?"

"My followers," remarks the King, "while vicious as temple dogs, are continually blind drunk and intractable."

Nightingale pours the rice wine. "In a dark street, even the lamp of a glowworm is welcome. How large is your following?"

"I have three such worms as you describe, whose glow at present brightens the gutter outside."

"Armed?"

"Should one of them bite a man, no medicine could save him."

"Tomorrow night, at the warehouse of Art Dealer Chang."

"I promise nothing. However, if you hear a rat scratch three times in the wall..."

Art Dealer Chang leads the way, rickshaw winding through a succession of muddy side streets. Nightingale follows, smoking a foul Chinese cigar. His throat is dry; he has only half of Chang's money.

The houses are fire-burned brick, crouching by the river. Above the rooftops, in the far distance, the White Dagoba of the Emperor glows faintly in the dark. The art dealer's rickshaw stops, by a long low building jutting over the water.

Nightingale tosses his cigar in the street. Ridiculous for a lone man to go into such a place.

"The sky lantern smiles on our endeavor." Art Dealer Chang flourishes a sleeve toward the moonlit water, takes out a key in the same movement, and opens the door.

Nightingale steps from his rickshaw, follows Chang into the echoing darkness. The art dealer lights a lamp, proceeds down an aisle of ornate dressing screens, whose painted birds and deer seem to move in the dancing flame. Nightingale darts his eyes nervously along the aisle, as a single disconcerting bead of sweat trickles down his arm. He would dearly love to blow the back of Chang's head off, but the officers, the gentlemen, the knights of the Rhine in his conscience weigh against him; he tries to convince them he's only a Berlin gangster, but they dazzle him with the Order of the Black Eagle, the Red Eagle, the Elephant, and the Seraphim.

Chang hangs his lamp, points to a panel depicting the outer pillars of a city wall. "Some people say—the pillars of Wu could walk."

Nightingale begins a gentleman's comment, but two shadows, large as the proverbial pillars of Wu, step from behind the screen and walk up his back. He listens, hopefully, for the scratching of a rat in the wall, instead is knocked through it, into a roomful of statuary. He manages to draw his automatic, only to have it kicked expertly out of his hand, along the floor.

The floor is warped, statuary crumbles around him, arms cracking off, among which he prays his own aren't numbered, but his head must still be on, for somebody's beating on it with wild animal cries.

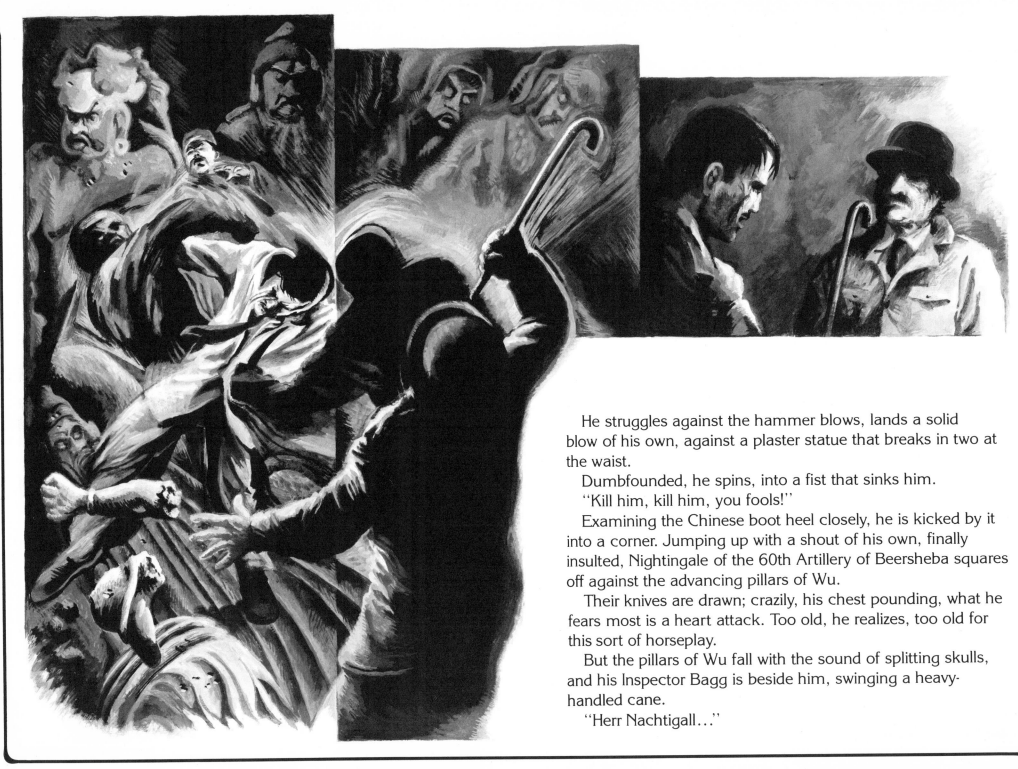

He struggles against the hammer blows, lands a solid blow of his own, against a plaster statue that breaks in two at the waist.

Dumbfounded, he spins, into a fist that sinks him.

"Kill him, kill him, you fools!"

Examining the Chinese boot heel closely, he is kicked by it into a corner. Jumping up with a shout of his own, finally insulted, Nightingale of the 60th Artillery of Beersheba squares off against the advancing pillars of Wu.

Their knives are drawn; crazily, his chest pounding, what he fears most is a heart attack. Too old, he realizes, too old for this sort of horseplay.

But the pillars of Wu fall with the sound of splitting skulls, and his Inspector Bagg is beside him, swinging a heavy-handled cane.

"Herr Nachtigall…"

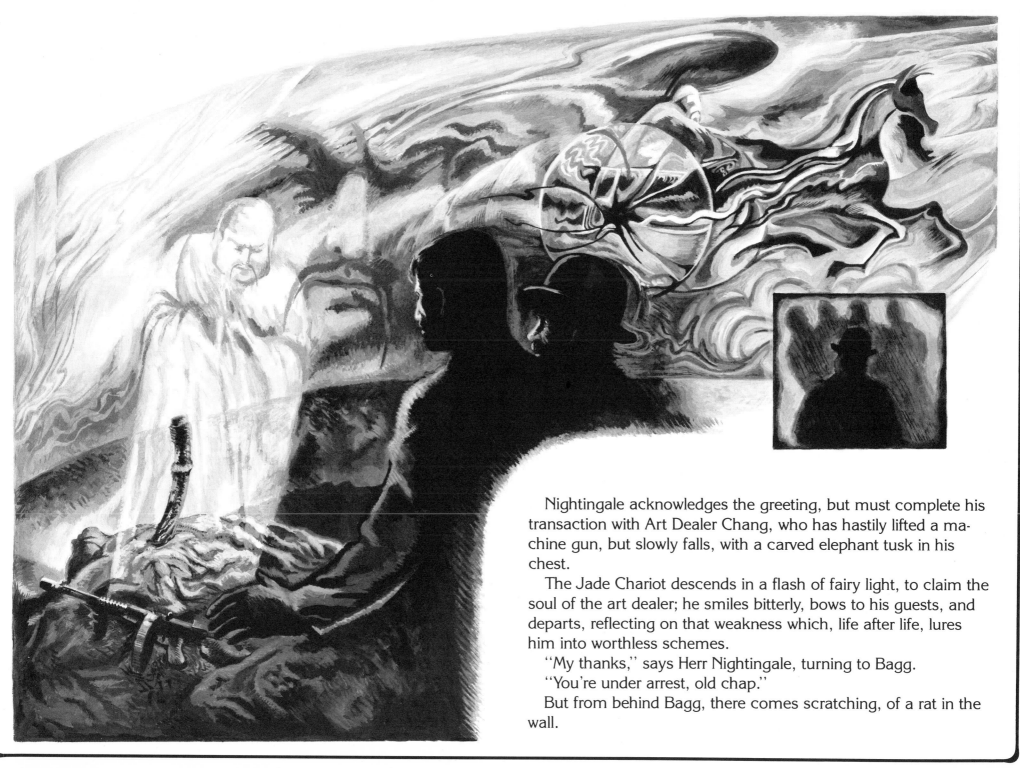

Nightingale acknowledges the greeting, but must complete his transaction with Art Dealer Chang, who has hastily lifted a machine gun, but slowly falls, with a carved elephant tusk in his chest.

The Jade Chariot descends in a flash of fairy light, to claim the soul of the art dealer; he smiles bitterly, bows to his guests, and departs, reflecting on that weakness which, life after life, lures him into worthless schemes.

"My thanks," says Herr Nightingale, turning to Bagg.

"You're under arrest, old chap."

But from behind Bagg, there comes scratching, of a rat in the wall.

"I don't want him harmed." Herr Nightingale points to Bagg's unconscious form.

"As you wish." The Beggar King puts away his blackjack.

"He'll need transportation to Dragon Harbor," says Nightingale. "But it should be a slow passage."

"I have a cousin who plies a houseboat along the waterway, with the slowness of eternity."

The low rumbling of a motor terminates their talk. Nightingale steps from the warehouse, onto the dock, swinging Art Dealer Chang's ornamental lamp. The motor answers with a surge; a large junk comes out of the shadow of the wharves, into the moonlight, and glides slowly in against Chang's dock.

"Nightingale, is that you?"

Nightingale answers, and a line thumps down at his feet.

The junk is made fast, and the machine guns loaded. The captain of the junk chats with Nightingale, inside, near the bodies of Chang and his fallen pillars.

"Bit of a to-do, I see."

"Nothing serious."

"Beggar King and his boys came through, did they?"

"In a manner of speaking."

"I told you they were good in a pinch." The captain glances around the warehouse. "Frightful amount of rubbish in here. Who's that you've tied in the corner?"

"Inspector Bagg of Scotland Yard."

"Smells of ginger. Are we sinking him?"

"He's for the Beggar King."

"Ah. Well, let's get a move on, shall we? The police launch is due by soon."

Bagg awakes in a sampan. His head is pounding. Beside him on the floor is a pig. Outside the matted cabin, the owner poles the craft along, singing of bean cake.

"And have you enjoyed the elegant illusions of our city?" asks the pig.

"If you don't mind," Bagg replies, "I'm rather tired."

Nightingale's junk is halted by a river demon. The sands, obeying the demon's command, hold the vessel fast. Nightingale, in no mood for games, draws his pistol, but the captain intervenes.

"My show, Nightingale."

"We can't afford delays."

"Agreed, but this fiend has relatives all up and down the river, and if you fire at it we'll have a hundred miles of fog so thick a blind man couldn't get through with a tin dog. So if you don't mind…"

The captain gives the order to let the fiend aboard. Nightingale retires to his deck chair. A woman with river weed in her streaming hair appears at the railing. The captain greets her with a courteous bow and leads her to his cabin, in which, presently, the light is extinguished.

A dense fog slowly wraps itself around the junk. The woman's laughter echoes within the cabin. Everywhere on deck is the sound of water dripping musically, as if from the throat of a songbird. Nightingale sits nervously, fearing the river police of Dragon Harbor, who bear no love for smugglers.

The laughter increases, accompanied by the captain's occasional whisper. The decks of the ship grow too slippery to walk on, and a yellow parasol floats past Nightingale's chair, drops of water falling off its spinning ribs.

Then armloads of fog cover the junk, until the air is insufferable. Through it, from across the water, Nightingale hears his name called, over and over. *"Don't answer,"* whispers the mate, crawling past Nightingale's chair.

"What the devil's going on?"

"'Appens all the time at this spot. A bit tricky, you know. But the skipper 'andles it."

From within the cabin now, there is only the sound of a woman's heavy breathing. From the river comes the sound of the Dragon Harbor police launch.

Nightingale stands on the treacherous deck, lurches toward the captain's cabin. The door opens before he's fallen three times, and the woman sweeps out, gliding effortlessly past him to the rail. The captain, wearing a bright robe embroidered with courting fishes, appears after her, in the doorway, and gives the order to start the engines.

The woman disappears over the side. The police launch fires a threatening salvo. Nightingale uncovers one of his machine guns.

"Here, watch this," says the captain, stepping beside him.

The fog rolls back like a curtain, revealing the police launch not a boat length away. The Chief of the River Police rides on an ornate chair fastened to the deck, a megaphone in his hand. As he raises it to his lips, a large-eared child with red claws steps from the mist and hovers over the water.

"A wine jar filled with treasure floats on the river," he cries toward the launch. *"Does no one wish to claim it?"*

The Chief of Police performs three trembling prostrations toward the child of the mist, throws paper money on the water, and calls through his megaphone, "We're only poor fishermen, Your Majesty."

"Let me have your megaphone too," says the child.

The sands that grip Nightingale's junk are scattered, stirred by rotten driftwood that dances round the vessel, setting it slowly free. The junk slips away, the fog closing up behind it and enveloping the stalled police launch again. But piercing the fog comes a woman's voice, calling through a megaphone, *"Nightingale, Nightingale,"* over and over.

Inspector Bagg lies in his sampan, watching the shoreline pass through matted slits. He is a serious man, frequently caught in ridiculous circumstances, he knows not why. Fate seems to lead him to them, as if to purify him with embarrassments.

On shore the crude huts pass in succession. Lone women rake the ground for fuel. The pig's father, a scholar with an independent turn of mind, has left his stamp upon his son, and thus the pig's commentaries on the passing landscape are edifying though, at times, obscure.

Collared Nightingale and lost him, reflects Bagg morosely. Takes the spots out of a chap.

I've half a mind to quit the case. Let some younger man have it, one of your five-day wonders from the College. And I'll have my ginger bath with Flo.

"In the correct season," says the pig, "a man may be maddened merely by striking him with such branches as you see growing there in the mud."

"Handy thing to know," responds Bagg gloomily.

"We're all the bean cake," sings the boatman, as he steers them along. Incense burns in a clay pot in the bow, for the water spirits of Dragon Harbor.

"Odd," says Bagg. "There's a megaphone floating on the water. I believe there's money stuffed inside it."

The sun has turned the river golden. They float toward the bend, plying with the other sampans. No boatman leans out for the megaphone, filled though it is, like a cornucopia.

The Satin Woman climbs the gangplank, the cricket cage on her finger. Within it, the cricket is rearranging his library, trying to immerse himself in things unrelated to her. But in spite of himself he feels her emanation; his bookshelves grow hopelessly disordered.

She enters her stateroom, unpacks a few things, and opens his cage.

He hops out, finds himself on her dressing table, among the perfumes and lotions. He wanders through them, down an avenue of glass in a city of enchantments. Her pearls hang over a cosmetic tray; he hops along them, dizzy from scent and situation.

"Have you been to sea before?" she asks, removing her shoes.

"Yes," he answers, landing in a stack of bracelets. "I owned a small nutshell. It sank off the African coast."

He speaks with hesitation, hardly aware of what either of them is saying. The stateroom is small; her stockings fall over the arm of a chair.

"You know Africa then?"

She's in her dressing gown. He retreats to his cage, busies himself at his bookshelves again, and asks her to close the lid.

B ut in the dark he's different, when the moon comes through the porthole and he answers with melodies that make her body tremble.

I'm in good voice tonight, he thinks to himself.

She hears a creaking noise, like a trapdoor opening overhead, and suddenly her vision has expanded to startling peripheries. Frightened, perceiving a thousand varied aspects of the night converging, she walks dizzily to the cage, opens up the lid.

"It is your insect eye," replies the cricket. "Compound, ommatidial."

She sinks onto the bed, awed by the spectacle of fluid form that is the ceiling—a foreign substance, protean, seeming now immense, now minute, now embroidered with designs labyrinthian and divine.

"I've found the attar of dreams," she says, reaching for the wondrous stuff above her, bathing her arms in its play.

"Not surprising," says the cricket, "seeing as you were born in it."

"Am I just a dream?" she asks.

"Enjoy the view," he answers, leaping onto the bed beside her, and continuing his song.

She realizes that she's glowing, intermittently, from the abdomen. Luciferous, she flashes blue, green, and red for hours while the cricket sings, his song seeming to inspire her fire-flash—but he says not so, she herself makes the glow, with pigment and enzyme fine as the moonlight.

But then the fire-flashes cease without warning, and she grows sad. "What has happened?" she asks, wanting the glow.

"Your soul, in choosing its magic form, has decided against the firefly."

"But why?" she sighs. "It was so pretty."

"Perhaps," he says, hopping closer on the sheets, "it finds itself more attracted to the—cricket form?"

"Yes," she answers, "I want that very much."

"I shall sing—and you shall hear it in your legs."

"I already hear you there," she says, softly.

"We shall see." He resumes his music, praying for a consanguineous metamorphosis.

She feels it happening in an aerial region, just beyond her body, the formation of a finer form, whose stages proceed once again by the manifestation of light. But it's a thin light now, and thread-like, spinning round her through the night. Warmth pervades her, and signals enter her head in comb-like patterns, bringing visions of existence so delicious she stirs impatiently and works to penetrate her cocoon of light, while her mortal body sleeps below, insensate, dreamless.

Or, she asks herself, am I its dream?

Her soul-form breaks through its silken girdle; she emerges.

"Japanese moon moth!" wails the cricket. "We are estranged."

She flies around him, emitting her attractant. "We can make it work," she says, and flutters down beside him.

They circle and dance, but each movement in the mating flight must be precisely that of the other, must correspond exactly, and they do not know each other's code.

Their passion searches madly. The moon moth is in frenzy and the cricket is in tears, for he knows how impossibly intricate the password is.

He improvises, but across these boundaries no one goes.

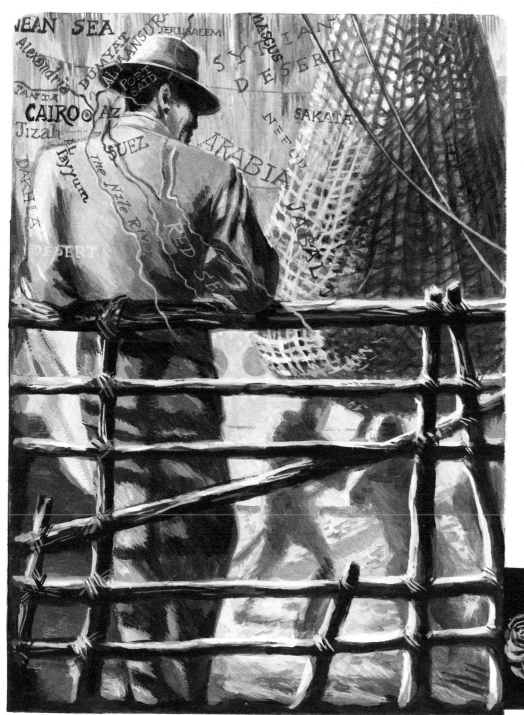

Nightingale's machine guns are transferred to the steamer *Eastern Star,* sailing for Egypt in three days. The Beggar King and his men break into the home of Art Dealer Chang, and find the attar of dreams.

The Beggar King's dream

The Satin Woman's wings are folded. She finds she cannot rise again. It's morning, the subtle colors of the night are gone, and her compound eye is closed.

She rests, and walks the deck, the cricket on her collar. But the memory of her maiden moon-flight lingers, and though she sees the iridescent blues no longer, she feels them down inside her, stirring an unsatisfied desire.

The sea wind blows her collar. The cricket takes refuge underneath it, where the invisible flowers of her perfume bloom and sway.

A bad mistake, he tells himself, to try and leap the gulf dividing us.

The Satin Woman takes a deck chair, beside an eager young man who's tried throughout the voyage to impress her with compliments and clever remarks. She smiles, but feels removed from coy deceptions.

The cricket wanders along her throat, the spring gone from his step. His path leads down twelve velvet stairs.

"May I get you a drink?" asks the young man. "Or some sort of tea?"

She shakes her head, but something in her suddenly limpid gaze, something in the way she slowly arches her back, leads the young man to believe his bright manner is finally breaking through to her.

The cricket wanders aimlessly along, antennae sweeping lightly over the softly scented slopes.

I'm fairly ravishing her with my charm this morning, thinks the young man, enthusiastically.

Inspector Bagg's boatman steers them through the junks and sampans clogging Dragon Harbor.

An appeal to the British Embassy is made. Bagg's countrymen, the wealthy and influential English of the port, do not let him down. With his pig and boatman he is put up in a pavilion overlooking the Embassy tennis courts.

It's more attention than Bagg cares for. Each afternoon he's taken to the racecourse, and afterward is forced to make polite conversation at a series of English-style garden parties. But by night his pig and boatman lead him through the city wall, beneath turrets and crenellated parapets, into the Old City. Here, among the gambling huts and pornographic peep shows, he breathes more freely.

She takes to wearing the cricket in her underwear. He roams freely there, in a melancholy affair hidden from her fellow passengers. It gives a distant quality to her conversation, which frequently falls into dreamy silence. She is thought by some to be a poetess. At times she faints without reason, a sudden little gasp taking her mid-sentence, her eyes glassing over, then fluttering wildly.

A few moments later, she is herself again.

But the insect dance is more complex than the human; as the moon moth she cannot find release, and the soul's dark trembling is denied her.

The cricket seeks counsel from a butterfly stowing away in the hold, who tells him, "Bend her antennae down. That always works."

Of course it doesn't work. The secret lies hidden, beyond gates of flame.

Nightingale aboard the *Eastern Star:* The ocean to his dreaming eye becomes the Sinai Desert, with cannons placed upon the waves and Von Kressenstein moving among the heavy artillery, showing himself to every man, and calling them by name.

The cannons smoke, and turn to foam. A dolphin leaps among the cavalry, and the long-dead campaign is just a wave in the unfathomable sea of memory.

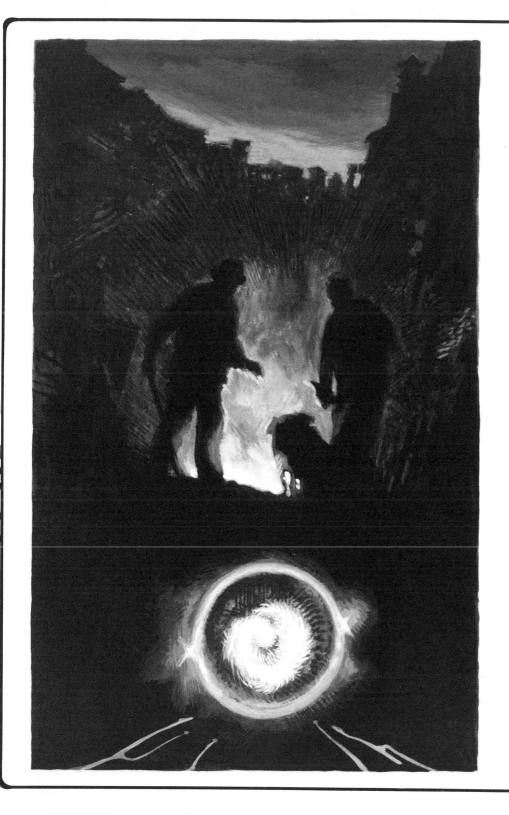

The back alley will lead them, explains the boatman, to a house of agreeable women. There might even be, he adds, a lady pig for the party.

"A hundred thousand rejoicings," murmurs the pig, whose scholarly pursuits leave him little time for the Interlocking of Tails.

The boatman stops to drink from their wine jug. Bagg swings along drunkenly through the muddy lane. His eyes chance to fall on a basket, tipped over in the mud. He rights it with his boot, is surprised by a sudden flash of light; the basket is filled with gold cups and candlesticks.

He looks up and down the alley. The wretched walls on either side are doorless; there is no owner in sight. He grasps the basket by the handle, lifts it from the mud.

The pig, smiling stupidly, flops toward him, belly full of rice wine and kumquats. But at the sight of a gold candlestick protruding over the edge of the basket, he hesitates; a dark page whirls up in his mind, from the pen of Tseu Lang, literary graduate at Ch'i-Cheu—a page dealing with men's hearts and the gift of gold one finds in the street.

He advances cautiously, peers into the basket, eyes drawn to the bottom of one of the shining cups.

"Ah!" He sits back in the mud, ears flattened, the experience of the unfortunate Tseu Lang ringing in them, Tseu of the Sung Dynasty, who found a basket such as this.

The boatman catches up, clutching the wall for support. Bagg holds out the basket. "I've found gold."

"A golden caterpillar!" wails the pig. "A golden caterpillar!"

The boatman looks into the basket. The caterpillar is nestled in one of the cups, its fur like an emperor's brocade, as if spun from the sun itself.

Bagg takes out a cup, holds it up and winks at the boatman. "A present for the ladies down the street, eh?"

"They won't accept it," says the boatman, his voice suddenly sober.

"And why not?"

The pig remains in the mud, eyes fixed on Bagg. It's clear to him now, as he sees Bagg holding up cup and candlestick, as he perceives the strange glow permeating Bagg's form—the English policeman has met himself in this alley.

For is it not written that he who finds the golden caterpillar has found the image of his own greed?

Her fellow passengers think it merely the cricket's conversation she enjoys, for the tiniest drop of gin and tonic sets him talking of golden caterpillars and red-and-white spiders with one missing leg.

Hopping up and down the bar, he babbles about fantastic insects—a cicada as large as a wastebasket, ant cities more beautiful than Rome, an insect who molts into human form for a single evening, taking the shape of a debonair gentleman who then calls on the lady of his choice.

He is something of an embarrassment to the Satin Woman, but the other passengers find it an amusing and cooling way to spend the afternoon, until the cricket collapses on a potato chip.

She carries him off in a tiny silver bell, the cricket clinging stupefied to the striker.

"I behaved badly again."

"My jewel-bug." Gently, she strokes his drooping antennae.

"Centipedes, two feet long…"

She opens the cabin door, carries him to her bed table. He stumbles around, singing to himself. He's been drinking too much lately, he knows it. But the affair isn't going smoothly, and their problem is profound.

The Satin Woman changes into something cooler and lies down. The tropic heat soon covers her with its burning breath. Restless, she tosses on the bed. The cricket leaps upon her ankle, and wanders there, in drunken circles.

She fears she has corrupted him. Assuring her he has always been a depraved insect, he staggers up her leg, toward the fine lace edge of her chemise.

"They won't accept a fine cup? Because of this little worm in there? I'll simply dump the beggar out."

Bagg throws the caterpillar in the street; it reappears a moment later, on the back of his hand. He removes it again and tramps it into the mud, only to have it return once more, unharmed, on his forehead.

"You have taken it in marriage," says the pig. "The cups and candlesticks are wedding gifts."

"From whom?" asks Bagg nervously, peeling the furry creature off his brow.

"From the previous owner, who wanted it no longer," says the boatman. He is no scholar, but the province of Szechwan is his home, and there fortune's gold caterpillar is known to all.

Bagg crushes the creature against the wall. As from a spider's woven sack, a dozen caterpillars wriggle out from under his thumb and crawl up his arm. He experiences a sudden fascination watching the little parade, feels rather full inside, as if he's just dined and smoked a good pipe. A glow spreads through his limbs, not at all the sort of thing you'd expect to feel with—bugs crawling all over you.

They crawl along his ears and eyebrows, under his hat and into his mustache; pleasant little feet actually, he observes with surprise. Somewhat soothing, you might say. "But see here, I can't appear like this in Government House."

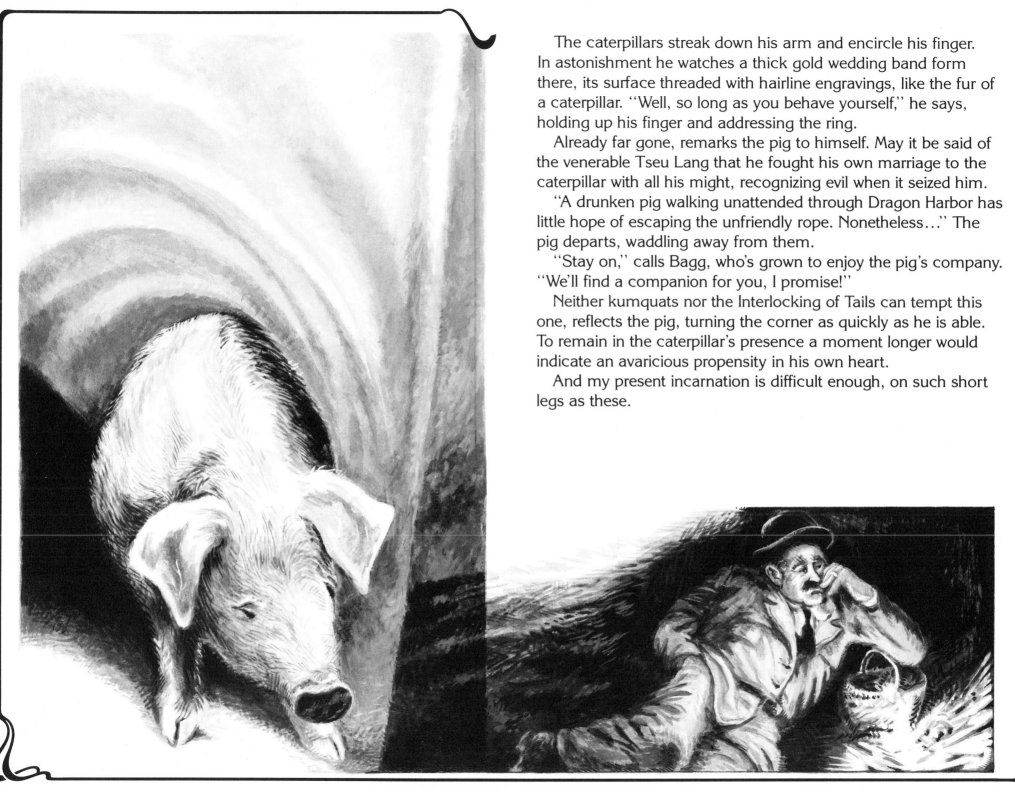

The caterpillars streak down his arm and encircle his finger. In astonishment he watches a thick gold wedding band form there, its surface threaded with hairline engravings, like the fur of a caterpillar. "Well, so long as you behave yourself," he says, holding up his finger and addressing the ring.

Already far gone, remarks the pig to himself. May it be said of the venerable Tseu Lang that he fought his own marriage to the caterpillar with all his might, recognizing evil when it seized him.

"A drunken pig walking unattended through Dragon Harbor has little hope of escaping the unfriendly rope. Nonetheless…" The pig departs, waddling away from them.

"Stay on," calls Bagg, who's grown to enjoy the pig's company. "We'll find a companion for you, I promise!"

Neither kumquats nor the Interlocking of Tails can tempt this one, reflects the pig, turning the corner as quickly as he is able. To remain in the caterpillar's presence a moment longer would indicate an avaricious propensity in his own heart.

And my present incarnation is difficult enough, on such short legs as these.

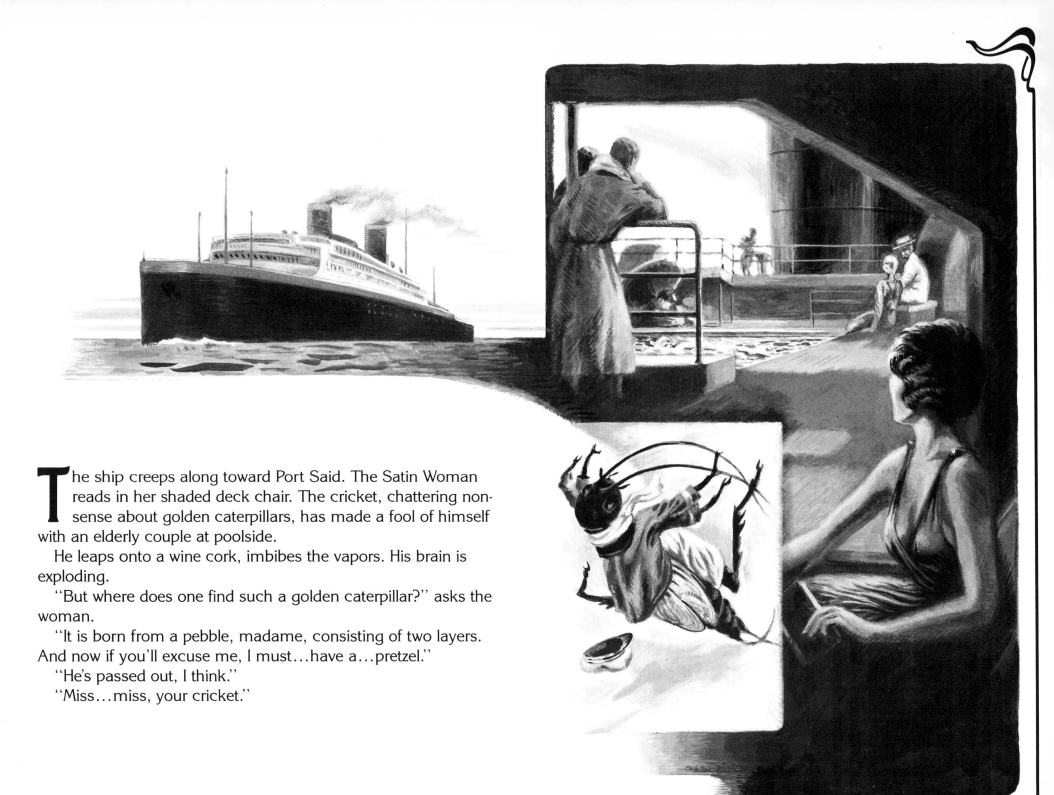

The ship creeps along toward Port Said. The Satin Woman reads in her shaded deck chair. The cricket, chattering nonsense about golden caterpillars, has made a fool of himself with an elderly couple at poolside.

He leaps onto a wine cork, imbibes the vapors. His brain is exploding.

"But where does one find such a golden caterpillar?" asks the woman.

"It is born from a pebble, madame, consisting of two layers. And now if you'll excuse me, I must…have a…pretzel."

"He's passed out, I think."

"Miss…miss, your cricket."

"You must feed it four inches of flowered silk from Szechwan each day."

"Rather expensive pet, wouldn't you say, old man?" Bagg adjusts the basket in the crook of his arm as they continue on through the alley. The thing to do with it, he decides, is turn it over to the local constabulary. Your lost-and-found, something of that nature.

"It will make you rich," explains the boatman. "Aside from the not invaluable gold dust it continually sheds from itself—" He pauses to collect a bit of it from Bagg's collar. "—it appropriates precious property from those around you."

Bagg feels a heaviness at his sleeves. Looking down, he observes that his cheap Chinese cuff links have been replaced by gleaming star sapphires.

The boatman smiles. "It will attend to your correspondence, your gardening, your housekeeping…"

"Not much call for that. However—" Bagg looks at his sleeve again, admiring the sapphire studs. "—the cut of these is acceptable. Yes, quite definitely."

A point of light flashes beneath his chin. Looking over his mustache, he discovers a large topaz adorning his tie.

"Extraordinary. Eh? Accessories popping out all over me?"

"The magic caterpillar grants what the heart desires." The boatman collects a bit more dust into his pouch.

"Magic. Yes…" A spectral fluttering disturbs the air around Bagg's head; leafy wings settle on his shoulder, beat softly; he hears the faint cry of a woman's voice lamenting something precious swallowed by the night. The wings cease beating, grow heavy.

The boatman picks the ornamental butterfly from Bagg's shoulder, presents it to him. It's made of polished horn, set with emeralds and rubies; two tiny diamonds glitter at the ends of the antennae.

Bagg, whose mind is generally steady but slow, experiences a sudden surge, by which he grasps at once the significance of hocus-pocus. It works, somehow. No one can tell him differently. Studs, tiepin, butterfly worth at least a thousand, depending on where you sell it.

. The caterpillar's a gold mine.

And I—I am its master.

In the city of Cairo, beyond the mosque of Mamluk Sultan El-Muayyad, in a street of whitewashed walls and closely grated windows, Herr Nightingale owns a house, and to it the Satin Woman comes.

The doorkeeper leads her through the sunless hall to her rooms. A cool fountain plays near the entranceway. The cricket cage is hung in a window facing the courtyard, in the shade of a line of sycamore trees.

She opens the cage. The cricket peers out, antennae trembling. "I could use a drink."

She mixes a drop of gin with chilled licorice juice, and they sit quietly, listening to the play of the fountain. But neither the white walls nor the fountain can keep the heat of midday out; she opens a latticed door, onto a sunken tub filled with rose water.

Floating on a rose petal, the cricket keeps her company while she soaks. He floats quite close to her eyes, and his fragile limbs fill her with love and sadness—he's little more than a leaf himself; how can he escape the heavy tread of time?

"I'm resilient, especially when I'm loaded. *Oh, fill the cup high, before life turns its back...*"

The water slowly drains from the pool; the rose petal sinks onto her belly, clinging like a kiss.

And I—I am its master.

Nightingale's serving girl taps lightly on the Satin Woman's door, enters with supper, finds her asleep.

Attracted by the bright cricket cage, the girl steps quietly up to it, peers inside.

A moth and cricket are within, in a tiny canopied bed.

Blushing deeply, the girl withdraws.

The cricket plays for her. The tune is bittersweet, filled with the echo of longing and the ashes of a misbegotten love; the melody touches lightly along her incompatible form, circles her combs and fades. If only, she thinks to herself, things could have worked out for us.

He looks up at her, a sad smile on his lips.

"And what, precisely," asks Bagg, "is my part of the bargain?"

"You must sing to your caterpillar to keep it happy. At times, it will be necessary to scold it, as it is known to turn lazy. Periodically, you must let it kill someone. That is all."

"I see."

"Here is a fine fabric store. Your servant suggests you command him to buy a large bolt of flowered silk from Szechwan."

"Yes, I suppose we should have some of that." Bagg fishes out his wallet, finds it stuffed with new bills, over which a fine gold dust is laid.

The boatman enters the store. Bagg remains dazed on the street, watching the merchant rush about, bringing down his finest bolts of silk.

Remarkable, this magic. So authentic you can spend it.

He turns his gaze back to the Old City wall. Its dilapidated turrets and parapets are aglow, streaked with a fine gold light. In every direction gossamer treasures are appearing—silver webs of mist upon the street lamps, and rooftops necklaced in jewels, with diamond night birds flying over them.

"Do you see?" he asks, as his boatman comes out with the bolt of silk. Bagg points to the pearls falling from the moon.

The boatman sees only the lanterns of Dragon Harbor. The vision is for the golden gentleman alone.

"I daresay," remarks Bagg, "these are your wonders of Cathay."

The entry of Nightingale's arms into Egypt: Customs Inspector Abdul el-Kahira, known also as Abdul the Incorruptible, admits the Oriental artifacts with a sweep of his pen, inquiring of Nightingale's health, happiness, and prosperity. "A gentleman was asking for you. Concerning the movement of some hashish. I took the liberty of arranging an appointment. You are available…?"

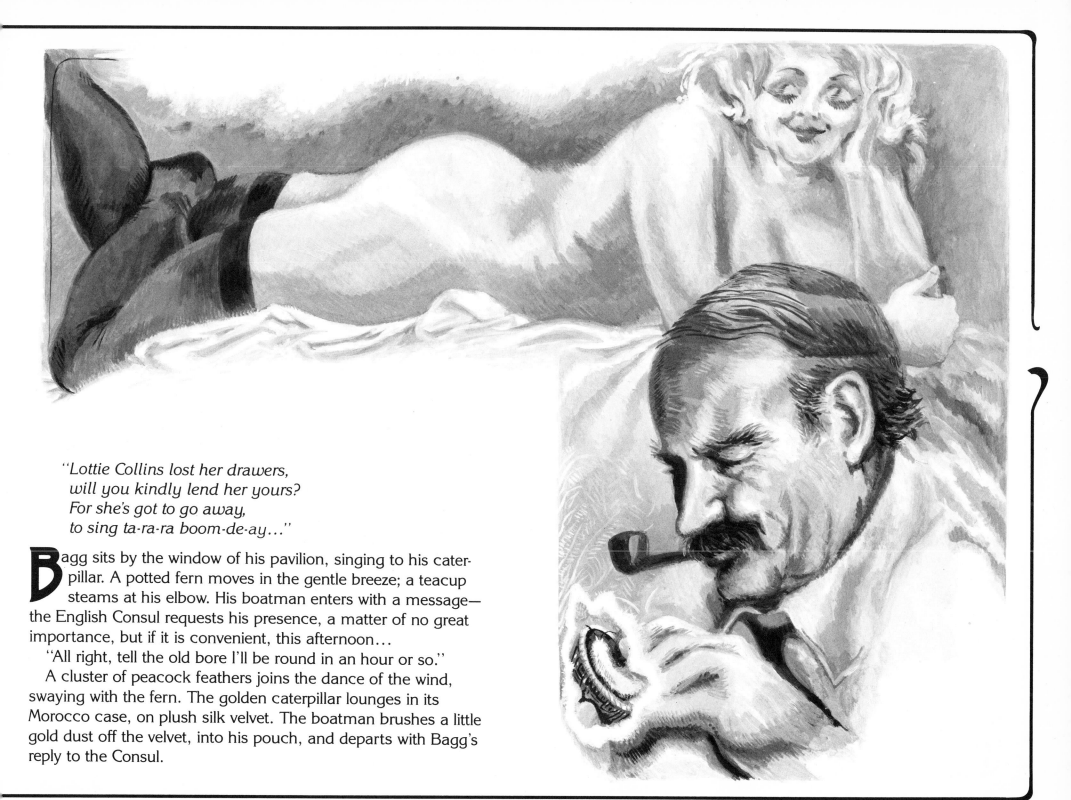

*"Lottie Collins lost her drawers,
will you kindly lend her yours?
For she's got to go away,
to sing ta·ra·ra boom·de·ay…"*

Bagg sits by the window of his pavilion, singing to his caterpillar. A potted fern moves in the gentle breeze; a teacup steams at his elbow. His boatman enters with a message—the English Consul requests his presence, a matter of no great importance, but if it is convenient, this afternoon…

"All right, tell the old bore I'll be round in an hour or so."

A cluster of peacock feathers joins the dance of the wind, swaying with the fern. The golden caterpillar lounges in its Morocco case, on plush silk velvet. The boatman brushes a little gold dust off the velvet, into his pouch, and departs with Bagg's reply to the Consul.

"**Y**es, Bagg, have a seat. Sherry? I'll come straight to the point. You're the most ungrateful wretch I've ever had the misfortune of knowing."

The Consul pauses. Bagg is dumbfounded. His personality does not usually elicit such reactions. Ungrateful? I attended their confounded garden parties, didn't I?

He moves uncomfortably in his chair. "I'm afraid—I don't understand."

"Don't you?" The Consul leans forward at his desk, seems about to spring across it, then drops back into the depths of his chair. A breeze from the window lifts a bit of gold dust from Bagg's lapel, carries it through a sunbeam where it dances for a moment, then falls lightly, into the Consul's wineglass.

The tiny flecks floating on the surface of his drink go unnoticed by the Consul; perhaps he thinks them a natural residue. He puts the glass to his lips, samples its contents with a distracted air, looks back at his visitor. "Give up the jewels and money, Bagg, and arrange to leave Dragon Harbor by the next boat. You had an unpleasant time of it in a sampan; very well, it has left you somewhat unhinged. Do you understand? I've told no one of the affair. I've no wish to press the matter further. You may begin with my sapphire cuff links. Just lay them on the desk, if you would, please. And my tiepin, that's an unusual topaz, not the quartz variety. My wife's butterfly—you haven't sold it yet, have you? And what of the money? The amount was not trifling. What I fail to see—what rather astounds me—is why you have flaunted the theft before my eyes. It's that part of the business which inclines me to be lenient. The man's lost his nerve, that has been my conclusion…that has been…my considered…"

The Consul seems to have difficulty breathing. His voice fails and the color drains from his face. His entire body sags, but his eyes, growing wider, remain fixed on Bagg. "My god…you've… but how could you have…poisoned me…"

He falls forward, clutching the edge of his desk, eyes suddenly eloquent with understanding. He tries to rise, in order to drag Bagg down with him, but a caterpillar crawls out of his nose and he collapses, half rolling under his desk.

Bagg kneels, tilts the head back. The pupils are already black, enormous, flecked with gold. He lets the Consul drop under his desk and considers his next move carefully. Circumstances have gotten the jump on him again.

ightingale rejoins the Satin Woman, gives her Chinese
brooches, rings, an antique mirror. "Belonged to a Han
wizard, or so I was told. Lovely setting, isn't it…"

Her face is blurred, distorted by the old discolored glass, but
she knows it is a true reflection of her troubled feelings. She
says nothing of the cricket, of the ache in miniature in her heart.
Presently the blinds are drawn, the lamp extinguished, and
Nightingale speaks softly. She answers him, in the old way,
and finds unexpected shelter from her tangled emotions, in his
familiar arms, in his rough low voice, in the murmured sounds
they make together.

The cricket hears, and slips quietly past the reunited lovers,
his head heavy, and no song left to sing.

But his attempt at a casual exit fails, as her courtship signal
reaches him and fills him with despair, for all that was, for what
they had; misshapen though it was, it was a world, a time, a
place for his heart to swell. Why, why, he cries, leaping to the
windowsill.

And—I should have known; in fact, did know, from the start.
But fate decides always, and we are its fools.

He drops into the courtyard. Her signal pursues him, the
sound of the moon moth, into the trees.

He hops away; her silhouette is everywhere, moon moth and
mortal, haunting his path.

He leaps to the courtyard wall, points his feelers about for a
direction. His legs shift nervously, a scratchy music coming
from them, of which he is unconscious.

The Satin Woman hears the tune: the tongue of crickets is her own.

The cricket leaps into the adjacent courtyard. I'll travel on, living in backyards. An insect doesn't need a roof over his head, or gin and tonic, or pretzels.

The Consul is stiffening beneath his desk. Bagg looks about the room, notices the objects in it peculiarly animated. The Consul's gold watch chain, to which a pearl-handled knife is fastened, rises from the Consul's body and floats in the air in front of Bagg. A tray of loose change on the desk begins to rattle, the coins dancing up and down. Bagg passes his hand over the tray and the coins oscillate violently.

A black onyx ashtray begins spinning on the Consul's desk; a gold cigar cutter follows suit. The caterpillar crawls up the leg of the desk and sits on a trembling silver inkwell, looking at Bagg, while the articles in the room jump about.

"See here," says Bagg, "I can't lug all this stuff away, even if you do mean to give it to me."

The caterpillar shrugs indifferently. The rattling valuables begin to whirl together in a ring. A woman's jewel box comes through the open window and from it spill bangles, bracelets, chokers, necklaces, all sparkling with precious stones, all joining the whirl-pool, whose center is a single glittering diamond. The other gems circle it like planets with their attendant moons, finally falling into it, making one shining central sun which shoots into Bagg's forehead and disappears.

He stands, baffled, with a headful of jewels. The less valuable objects in the room settle back into place.

"All right," says Bagg to his caterpillar, "but what about the body?"

The Consul stirs beneath his desk, struggles back into his chair, pupils still enormous, face still waxen, but a bit of color returning to his lips. "I shall give the semblance of life…until your boat has sailed."

"I say—" Bagg steps up to the desk. "I *am* sorry for this. It's the beastly caterpillar—has a mind of its own."

"I…am…the caterpillar." The Consul smiles grotesquely, his former arrogance returning, along with his cutting manner, but the eyes of the man are dead as his black onyx ashtray, except for the wriggling pulse of gold at the center, where his ghoul is lurking. To these gold points Bagg addresses himself.

"You're some sort of—demon, are you?"

"Of the intermediate rank."

"All those jewels you stuck in my head—I feel them juggling about in there."

"A temporary measure. You must leave Dragon Harbor at once. I can support this body for no more than a day."

The Consul rings for his secretary. The secretary enters and Bagg withdraws down a long hallway and onto the porch, noting that the Consul's sapphire cuff links have disappeared from his wrists, along with the topaz from his tie. Upon closing his eyes, he sees them shining inside his skull, among the other gems and stones.

Gives rather the effect of a chandelier.

He walks along, reflecting on the Consul. The old boy's hands were undoubtedly muddy; how else could he have afforded sparklers like that? It's the climate out here; sheer weight of history corrupts. I believe the pig spoke at length on it. I, dozing, on the water. Caught some of it. Pity the pig didn't stay on. Nice little chap.

Bagg navigates the crowded street, the jewels flashing fragments of conversation in his brain, odds and ends, lawn-party stuff, bits of Embassy gossip that cling to them.

The cricket finds a niche for the night in a brick overlooking a moonlit pool. The Satin Woman's signal has ceased, but he needs a drink badly. Upon the surface of the pool a water strider dances ecstatically. The cricket watches the entrancing movements, remembering again, slowly, what it is to be an insect—the incomparable lightness of it all!

Humans are so heavy, the spirit chained down in them, unable to leap or fly, while I—he leaps to the edge of the pool—I—

need that woman so.

Nightingale's carriage makes its way through strings of camels, government clerks on donkeyback, water carriers, sugarplum salesmen, children at play. The Satin Woman sits beside him; her veil sets off her dark eyes and hides the confusion at her mouth. She thinks of the cricket and calls to him silently, to the tiny lover lost in the ancient city. The jewel-bug is stuck in her heart. Drops of sadness fall continually, yet something says *Nightingale, Nightingale,* over and over, where the drop falls.

"Gospodinoff is a Greek, but they've closed him out of business there. He has to bring his hashish in from Turkey now. So he needs us." Nightingale taps on the carriage wheel. The driver turns down a private lane, to a palace of sorts—marble balconies, inlaid archways, shaded by the drooping crown of date palm trees.

They enter through a heavy door, inconspicuously guarded, are shown down a long carpeted hallway, into Gospodinoff's study.

The floor mosaic, set in marble, draws Nightingale into cool star-woven spaces. The Satin Woman is tired, removed; the ostentatious wealth of Gospodinoff's house does not seduce her. She's thinking of the cricket, his tiny heart—no bigger than a mustard seed, and of his blood—could it be more than a single drop?

"Well, Nightingale—" The host settles himself onto a midnight-blue divan. "—how are you going to move the cargo?"

"The Army." Nightingale puts a small chunk of iced melon to his lips.

"The Army?" Gospodinoff chuckles. "Have you dealt with them before?"

"Frequently."

Gospodinoff nods, drums his fingers on his protruding stomach. "A military transport…" He looks up, smiling. "How do we proceed?"

"The hashish is moved as rations."

"Two tons at a time?"

The Satin Woman explains her connection with the Corps d'Armée, through a certain transport officer, who is for sale, in the neighborhood of a thousand lira. Gospodinoff allows his eyes to drift over the outline of her body within its loose-fitting gown.

Nightingale can see she's distracted by something; still, she's the perfect one for the job. And she is, of course, his destiny. She is, as they say, written on his forehead.

Gospodinoff sips his coffee, continues admiring Nightingale's colleague. He's happy to have them in his organization, happy indeed, and as he casts his eyes along her legs his heart gives off one of its irregular palpitations. Distressing; some foods, certain women. But it is the arena of life, is it not? Heart fluttering, he leans forward, asks if he might read the lines of her palm.

Transport Major Medjid dines with the Satin Woman, alone, in Istanbul, in sight of the waters of the Golden Horn. He would be delighted to assist her in the little escapade, gallantry alone would dictate his answer; payment should be in gold coin, of course. Is she interested in a few hundred Ethiopian slaves as well? No? A pity, the business is flourishing at the moment. Eunuchs, perhaps? Outmoded field artillery? Would she care for five dozen camels, bred especially for speed and silence—a smuggler's dream, at only a thousand English pounds apiece.

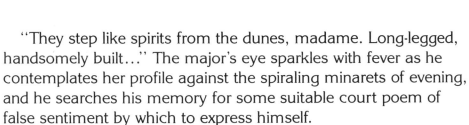

"They step like spirits from the dunes, madame. Long-legged, handsomely built…" The major's eye sparkles with fever as he contemplates her profile against the spiraling minarets of evening, and he searches his memory for some suitable court poem of false sentiment by which to express himself.

"First shipment will be two tons."

"Yes, yes, two tons, twelve tons, whatever you like. Do you know the poem of Fuzuli, of the love-drunk nightingale?"

"And how does that go?"

"Upon the thorn's point, he dies for love of the rose."

The Satin Woman explains the details of the operation, in which Major Medjid shows no interest, but she knows that he listens with close attention and, as in the past, will oversee everything without error; and that before evening is spent, he will several times propose their making love.

How clumsy men seem to her now, their ritual so crude. Major Medjid's gestures, his little jokes, his cologne, cannot compare to the abdominal lights, the ravishing wings, the maddening attractants she has known.

But perhaps he might accidentally speak the right word, or a word might catch in his throat and fill her with a sudden tenderness for him; it is all possible, and Major Medjid, sensing this, presses on, desperately, blindly, ordering more wine, quoting other four-line stanzas, and twisting the end of his nose.

The cricket sits near the front of a carpet shop, listening to the philosophers argue the nature of existence under the shade of the awning, while birds of the quarter swoop down, picking off buzzing gnats and camel flies.

Hidden in the shadows, the cricket is out of harm's way. The sidewalk beyond the shop is covered with bird droppings. One of the droppings moves.

The cricket watches it carefully, sees it move again, close by the table of philosophers, where the soul and secret of life are being delineated.

The birds come in low, the dropping freezes, is but one among many others, discarded and unappetizing to the birds, who eat the bright-winged camel flies and speed away.

Tiny legs extend from the dropping and again it moves, beneath the chair of a philosopher.

"Here now," says the cricket softly, "I see that you are walking."

"And so it is," replies the dropping. "Indeed, I have been walking all morning."

"This is new to me," says the cricket.

"But old to me," answers the dropping, revealing his eyes and mouth.

The philosophers continue their discussion of the celestial melon and the illuminated script. The cricket takes a hop toward the dropping and finds a bug, not terribly different from himself, except for the strange markings which perfectly simulate a bit of bird excrement.

The birds return, the cricket leaps out of danger. The other insect lies still, arms and legs indrawn, and once again is indistinguishable from the droppings on the stones.

"This is most enlightening," remarks the cricket.

"The secret of life," says the other insect, "is to look like a piece of shit. One need know nothing else."

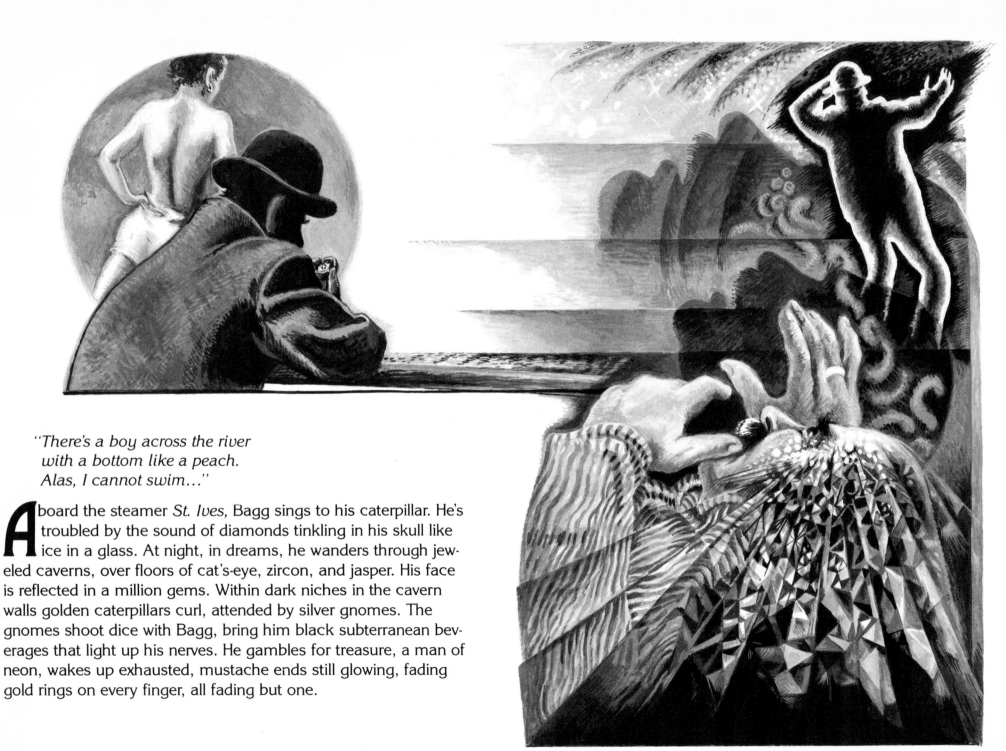

*"There's a boy across the river
with a bottom like a peach.
Alas, I cannot swim…"*

Aboard the steamer *St. Ives,* Bagg sings to his caterpillar. He's troubled by the sound of diamonds tinkling in his skull like ice in a glass. At night, in dreams, he wanders through jeweled caverns, over floors of cat's-eye, zircon, and jasper. His face is reflected in a million gems. Within dark niches in the cavern walls golden caterpillars curl, attended by silver gnomes. The gnomes shoot dice with Bagg, bring him black subterranean beverages that light up his nerves. He gambles for treasure, a man of neon, wakes up exhausted, mustache ends still glowing, fading gold rings on every finger, all fading but one.

In Istanbul the horses wear necklaces to ward off the evil eye. The Satin Woman relies on a thin gold ferronnière, its single moonstone dotting her forehead with light. She wanders the streets among the traders and peddlers, drinks thin lemonade. Her business arrangements are in motion, and she has time for herself on the shimmering pavement, alone in the great city.

She enters the Old Market. Amidst it all, the vast array of Oriental goods and the talk of the merchants, she feels the solitude that has grown in her by degrees. All others seem hypnotized by human relationships, and by the things they own or seek to own.

It whirls about her like a sandstorm, the glittering bits of the shattered world she no longer seems to share.

Has the cricket done this to me, she wonders.

Some heavy illusion has fallen from her. She feels the form of the moon moth with her. Men's games and the languors of the harem, men's lies and the marketplace, no longer fascinate her.

What is left?

The distillate of her solitude, dripping from the heart-pin. It drips and the moon moth drinks. Can anyone deceive her now?

Nightingale, Nightingale, proclaims the pool below, where the heart-pin is reflected, in ripples, with each drop.

The street poets and musicians sense something as she passes, the moon moth's wings fanning the candles in their brain. A shoe cleaner, sitting in the shade of a doorway, feels the urge to shine the sun as she goes by, and he drags after her, filled with wonder.

She stops at the stall of a letter writer, who touches his tarboosh and offers the services of love, cut-rate, on perfumed paper.

An impassioned communiqué, filled with moonlight and sighing, is composed.

"To whom, dear madame, shall I address it?"

To the cricket who is gone? To Nightingale? To Major Medjid?

"To the Golden Horn," she says softly, pointing to the water.

The shoe cleaner grasps the envelope. "I shall deliver it." He is a Turk, and knows the meaning of a love letter flung in the sea.

The Satin Woman walks on, along the white sheet of pavement, enjoying her secret solitude, followed by double sets of agents—those of Gospodinoff and Major Medjid, professional shadows who eye each other suspiciously.

In the ship's lounge, Bagg sneezes. A ray of light shoots from his nose, solidifies a moment later in the frothing mug he holds, a mug now filled with jewels. Casually, he pockets the dripping gems and departs the lounge. His head is much cleared, though he detects rustling toward the back, as of a bat trapped in a chimney.

The deck is warm and bright. He walks to the ship's rail, stares at the water. His mustache tickles, he sneezes again, forgetting his position; the horn-and-ruby butterfly sails out of his nose, flutters desperately for a moment, and sinks, into the sea.

Bagg calls to the caterpillar who sleeps on his finger, but the demon is in a mood and refuses to wake.

A mermaid rises from the sea foam, the butterfly in her hair. She blows a kiss to Bagg and swims away, arranging her streaming coiffure around the glittering pin.

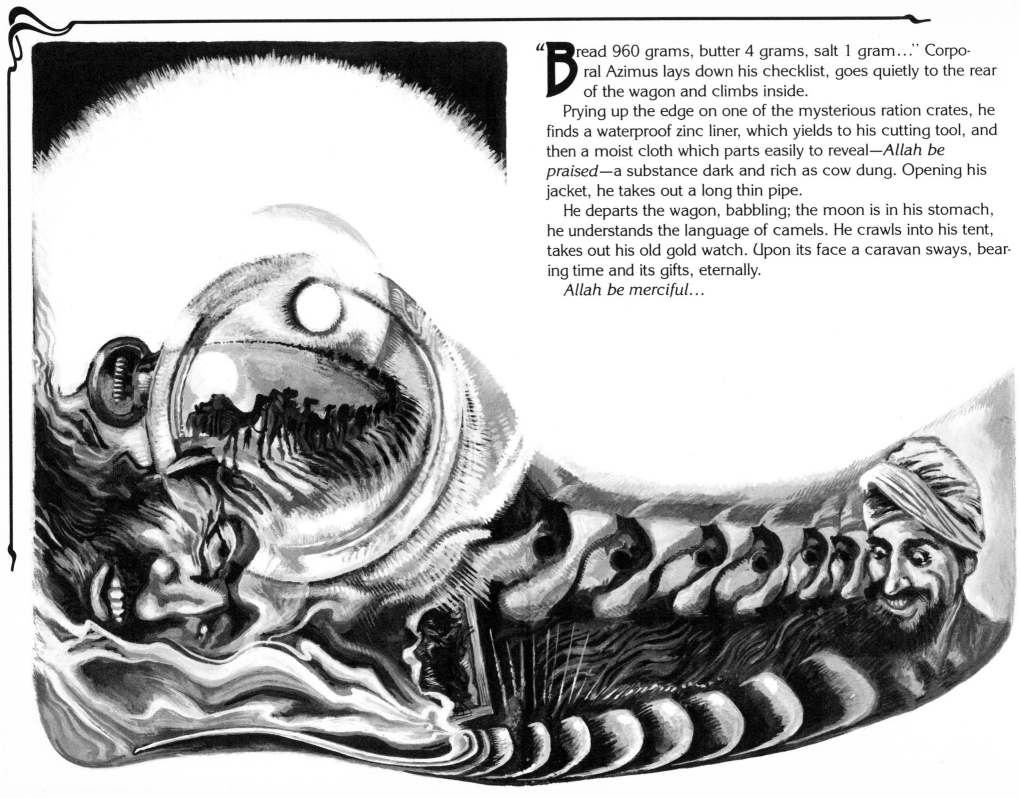

"Bread 960 grams, butter 4 grams, salt 1 gram…" Corporal Azimus lays down his checklist, goes quietly to the rear of the wagon and climbs inside.

Prying up the edge on one of the mysterious ration crates, he finds a waterproof zinc liner, which yields to his cutting tool, and then a moist cloth which parts easily to reveal—*Allah be praised*—a substance dark and rich as cow dung. Opening his jacket, he takes out a long thin pipe.

He departs the wagon, babbling; the moon is in his stomach, he understands the language of camels. He crawls into his tent, takes out his old gold watch. Upon its face a caravan sways, bearing time and its gifts, eternally.

Allah be merciful…

Bagg returns to the Yard, submits his report on Nightingale, and a request to be taken off the case. He has his ginger bath with Flo, who steps into it garbed in diamond necklace and bracelet.

I never took 'im for such a spender, she thinks, stirring up the bath. Certainly a cut above them other detectives been 'elpin' me out with young Stanley.

To Bagg the gift is nothing—he has hundreds more at home, in an ever-growing pile of stolen jewelry.

He sits in the steam with Flo, musing on his conflict of duty.

"I'm so 'appy you've returned, Geoffrey," says Flo shyly, dangling her bracelet over the water, and giving him a little kiss.

A wave of jewel thefts has hit London and he is, of course, behind them, with his caterpillar. A compromising position for a copper to be in, he reflects. And the Policeman's Charity Minstrel coming up. How can I sing a song or two with the other lads? I can't even look them in the eye.

But the bloody worm's cured my rheumatism.

The tub is long and deep, and Flo is more attentive than she's ever been. Bagg sinks back into the water, feeling rather like a maharajah.

"**S**hine them, noble sir? Shine them like the sun?"
A passing government clerk looks down, sees dust on his shoes and yields to the shoe cleaner with a contemptuous gesture, which he practices whenever possible, in order to prepare for rise in the Ministry. The shoe cleaner opens his box, the most festive in all Istanbul, painted, mirrored, ornate as a king's saddle. Of possessions he has no others, and needs none. The shoe box contains all, the universe and its stars, among his rags and tins.

"Yes, master, an extraordinary shine for thee, a shine in which marvels shall appear..." The shoe cleaner is unusually agitated. The memory of the Satin Woman is still with him. The way she walked—the street itself had shifted excitedly, and he'd felt something flutter around the fire of his shoe cleaner's heart, around the shining lamp within him, from which his spirit stirred out of a deep and ancient sleep.

A most unusual lady, thinks the cleaner, brandishing his shoe cloth as never before.

The rag leaps, like a licking tongue of flame, exciting the magical propensities of the polish, quickening the sleeping surface of the leather.

The government clerk sweats into his tight collar, snarls at the cleaner, "Be careful of my cuffs."

"Cuffs? Cuffs? They shall never know what has happened beneath them. Yet later on—" The shoe cleaner smiles. "—they will hang gently, and lightly add the final touch."

He applies a few drops of water, anointing the reluctant shoe tip. The swirling clouds upon it part, and a hidden sun flashes for a moment in the leather.

The clerk looks at his watch, impatiently shifts his briefcase, which carries nothing but his initials on the outside, yet holds all his hopes for the universe and its stars. "Hurry it up, worthless dog."

"Yes, yes, I'm flying, master, over the depths." Again the secret sun flashes, and now the sacred garden has appeared in the shoe tip. Wish-fulfilling trees sway in the magic light; a man need only look on them for his wildest dream to manifest.

The shoe cleaner steals a glance to see if the clerk has noticed; no, he is watching a shining Cadillac pass, with a faraway look in his eyes. Now he snaps his head back. "What are you muttering? What sort of fool are you?"

"The most foolish of fools, master." The shoe cleaner's rag draws the spark from the other shoe. If that woman could see work like this, to whom would her love letter be mailed? To whom, I ask you.

The spark spreads, the fire is fanned, the wish-fulfilling fountain appears in the tip of the shoe, with heavenly rays playing upon it. Tiny celestial maidens dance around it, enraptured by its play. Whoever glances at it, even casually, is given paradise on earth.

This, remarks the shoe cleaner to himself, is my absolute double-barreled best shine.

"That's enough," says the clerk, taking his foot away. "I haven't got all day."

"It should be sufficient, master," says the shoe cleaner slyly, waiting for the young man to spy his good fortune. The wish-trees gently bend in the right shoe tip, and the fantastic fountain is casting sun-filled drops of love from the left one.

But the clerk doesn't bother to look down. He is producing a superior air, which a man in politics must have if he wants to rise. "You call that a shine?" He stares in boredom at the sky, digs in his pocket for a coin, finds one, then finds a smaller one, and tosses it with scorn at the shoe cleaner. "That's no shine at all, my man."

"All things fade, master," says the shoe cleaner, as the Supreme Shine vanishes, leaving only a competent glow. The clerk sniffs, puts on his dark glasses, and walks away.

The shoe cleaner packs his box, moves to the shade of the doorway, lays his head against the up-raised shoe rest. A woman like that woman. Who strokes the lamp of a man's spirit. What miracles of light would be produced if I could but polish her toenails.

He closes his eyes, listens to the shoe rest, to which the soles of Istanbul have pressed the many secrets of the streets.

He hears the stumbling pilgrimage of the drunkards, the solemn march of the camels, the jerking footsteps of the mad. But the scuffling of her sandals is very far away.

Consulting the bits of broken glass attached to the side of his box, he finds her image moving in the fragments, from piece to piece, in an unfamiliar city.

Already she has gone, already departed from Istanbul. But I must go to her. I must seek her out and polish her toes.

He climbs upon his box, straddles the shoe rest, hangs on to the hinges. "Find her for me."

The box rises tentatively, flies a few yards along the sidewalk, and crashes down. "Up, up," urges the shoe cleaner. The box staggers a few more yards, lifts again, only to sink once more into the gutter.

Nightingale at his café: Abdul the Incorruptible outlines a plan for smuggling whiskey to the faithful.

"Through one of my associates in Customs House, a man as principled, aboveboard, and unsullied as myself, I have made contact with a buyer…"

Nightingale's eyes wander the tables, as the Incorruptible explains the necessary bribes, but Nightingale is weary of shadows, Turkish coffee, and baksheesh. His gaze moves along the beaded awning, and the sidewalk, where the peddlers push and pull their wares. Among them a sun-ruined man threads his way, with a bearing that mystifies Nightingale, for it is like his own, but broken, and the face as it comes closer is familiar, but twisted by fever, like something seen in a Han wizard's mirror.

"Rantzau, is it you?" asks Nightingale softly.

The memory rises up around them, of 5000 camels, 20,000 troops, moving out from Beersheba.

"...the whiskey itself is not fit to pour on a dog. We shall realize an excellent profit..."

"Nachtigall..."

Their memories meet, upon the sand, the moon two days past the full, a storm raging, the breeches of their rifles wrapped with rags. Ahead the British await their attack. All around in the whirling sands of this narrow camel track to Suez the ghosts of great armies watch—they too have labored here, with Ramses, Alexander, and Napoleon.

"...there are, as well, 1200 sun helmets of fresh manufacture..."

Rantzau smiles, extends his hand to Nightingale, the failed campaign written in both their palms, along the twisting trenches of the heart.

"...having only a small hole in the very center of each helmet, the most minor of defects..." Abdul the Incorruptible accepts all friends of Nightingale as his own, signals for the waiter. Rantzau speaks with hesitation, fumbles in his wallet for a photograph. Nightingale takes it, stares at the smiling faces, his own among them, but it is not this which speaks from the photograph. These soldiers, of a defeated artillery battery, are time itself.

The newspapers are filled with speculation on the Gold Dust Bandit baffling Scotland Yard. The grid book of every London police station has a page for him, marking one of his jobs. But his face does not appear in the portrait file; among those who should know, it is agreed they're dealing with a new man, and that is going to make things difficult.

"Never a sign of entry, and no marks anywhere, only the bit of gold dust sprinkled here and there. Gentlemen, he's making a mockery of us, and I want results." Detective Inspector DeWitt looks around the room at the men of his division. Bagg shifts nervously in his seat, listening to the reports of the other men, all of them trying to sound like they're onto something, all of them just blowing their horn.

Detective DeWitt speaks again, less caustically, implying there's promotion for the man who brings the Gold Dust Bandit in.

Bagg fights down the urge to arrest himself.

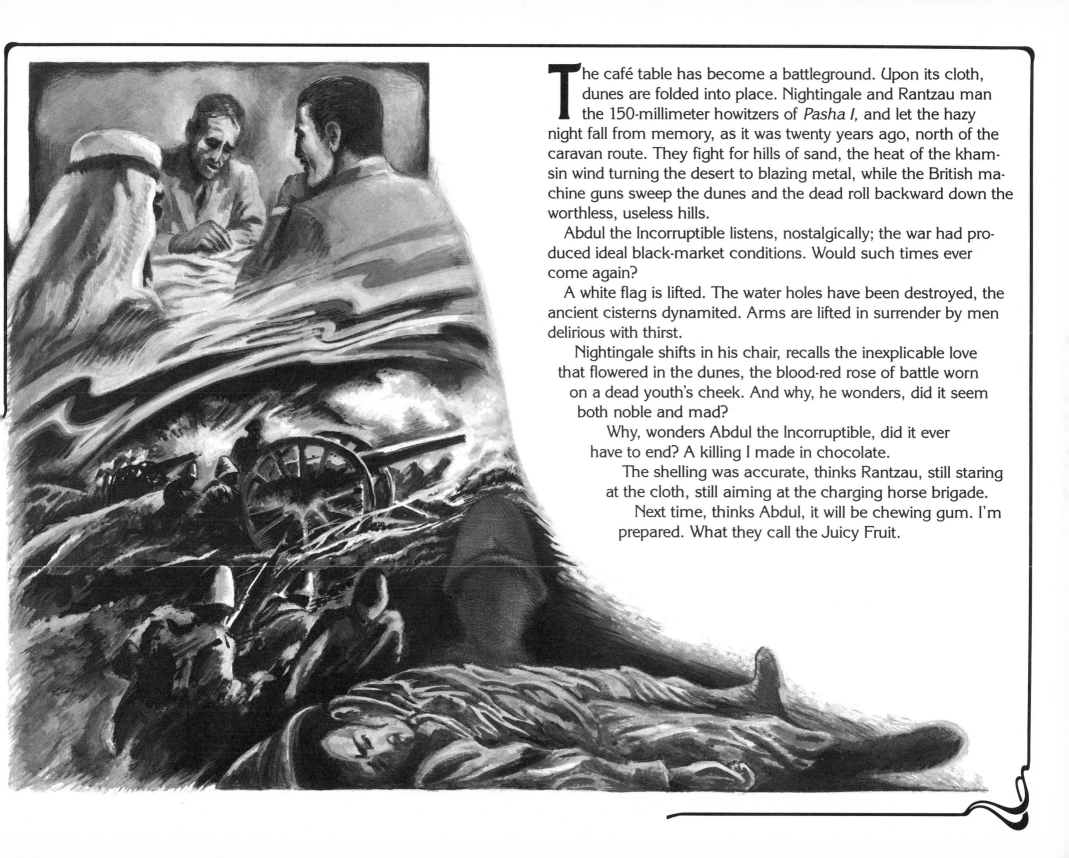

The café table has become a battleground. Upon its cloth, dunes are folded into place. Nightingale and Rantzau man the 150-millimeter howitzers of *Pasha I,* and let the hazy night fall from memory, as it was twenty years ago, north of the caravan route. They fight for hills of sand, the heat of the khamsin wind turning the desert to blazing metal, while the British machine guns sweep the dunes and the dead roll backward down the worthless, useless hills.

Abdul the Incorruptible listens, nostalgically; the war had produced ideal black-market conditions. Would such times ever come again?

A white flag is lifted. The water holes have been destroyed, the ancient cisterns dynamited. Arms are lifted in surrender by men delirious with thirst.

Nightingale shifts in his chair, recalls the inexplicable love that flowered in the dunes, the blood-red rose of battle worn on a dead youth's cheek. And why, he wonders, did it seem both noble and mad?

Why, wonders Abdul the Incorruptible, did it ever have to end? A killing I made in chocolate.

The shelling was accurate, thinks Rantzau, still staring at the cloth, still aiming at the charging horse brigade.

Next time, thinks Abdul, it will be chewing gum. I'm prepared. What they call the Juicy Fruit.

"You've got to ease off." Bagg addresses his caterpillar. His bureau drawers are stuffed with the oldest jewels in Great Britain, and the Big Four of the Yard are clamoring for an arrest. The papers now call it "the work of a first-class criminal mind."

"We can hide the jewels in your head," says the caterpillar, "if you fall under suspicion."

"I don't particularly like being a walking jewel box, if you don't mind. My sinuses are still acting up from the last time."

"I'll put them in your heart, then."

"I'll take them for you, boss," says the boatman. "Sell them for you quick."

"You'd be collared inside an hour," answers Bagg, with a sigh, staring down at his slippered feet.

I have to get the sparklers out of the country, to Antwerp, Amsterdam, Brussels, to receivers big enough to handle them, and do it without drawing attention to myself.

"You worry too much," says the caterpillar. "I'm protecting you."

"Then stop leaving gold dust all over everything!"

"It's essential to my digestive process."

Bagg sighs once more, and switches off the light. His career is finished, that's clear.

He sits in the dark, reminiscing, about daggers, nitric acid, obscure streets in North London, a beer shop in Houndsditch. He'd come up through the ranks, had struggled all the way, had potatoes thrown at him as well as knives, had been made to learn compound arithmetic and advanced English composition for promotion from sergeant to inspector—and here I sit, with a crooked caterpillar and a degenerate coolie.

The caterpillar begins to glow. "I'm getting a message about you. From the International Bureau. Nightingale has embarrassed the British Navy in the Mediterranean. You're being reassigned to the case."

Cairo, thinks Bagg. I can sell the swag to Gospodinoff.

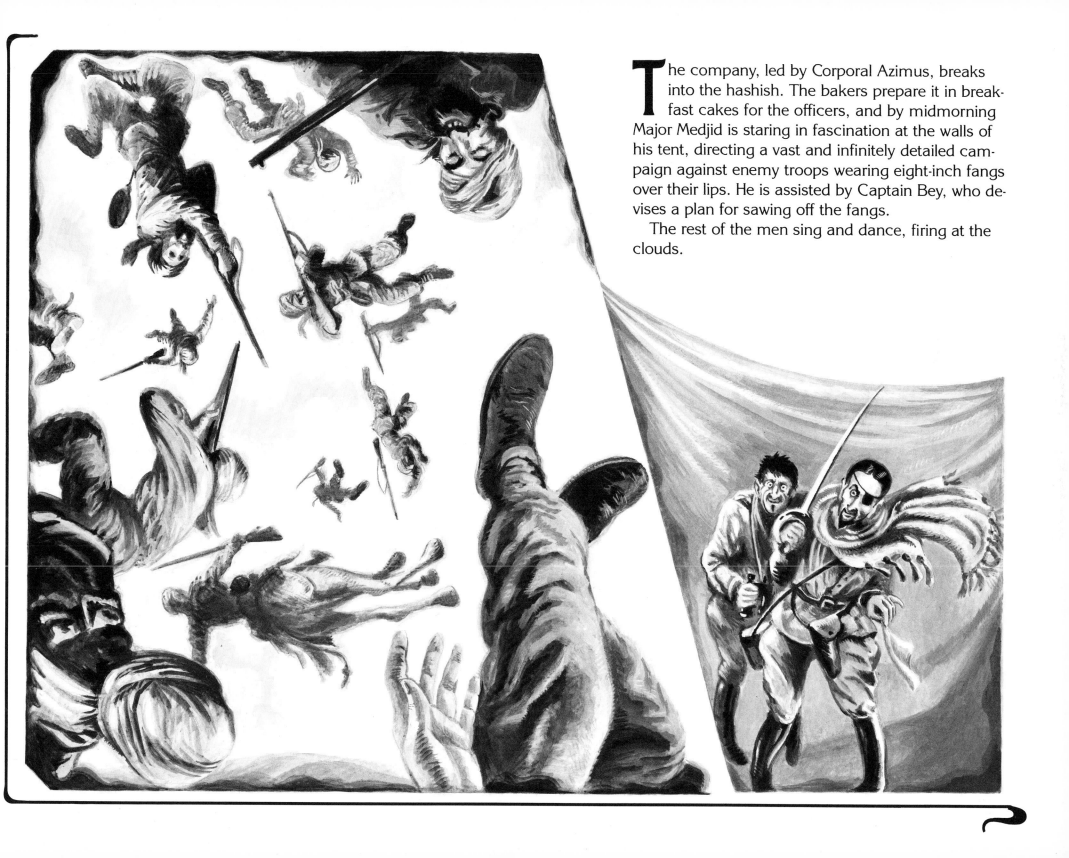

The company, led by Corporal Azimus, breaks into the hashish. The bakers prepare it in breakfast cakes for the officers, and by midmorning Major Medjid is staring in fascination at the walls of his tent, directing a vast and infinitely detailed campaign against enemy troops wearing eight-inch fangs over their lips. He is assisted by Captain Bey, who devises a plan for sawing off the fangs.

The rest of the men sing and dance, firing at the clouds.

"We don't expect you to return without Nightingale," says the Superintendent, "if it takes the whole of five years. Do I make myself clear?"

"Yes, sir."

The Superintendent puts a friendly arm on Bagg's shoulder, brushes a bit of goldish dust from his collar. "Have at him, then, and good luck to you. I know you'll take him this time."

Bagg departs England, his body stuffed with jewels. His joints ache, and his walk is stiff as a giraffe. He has difficulty speaking, must avoid the lounge, for his earlobes glow in the dark and light seems to come from his fingernails.

"A pretty mess."

"You are the embodiment of wealth." The caterpillar is chewing his flowered silk in a small porcelain dish.

Bagg tries to say more, but bracelets rattle against his uppers.

The Satin Woman enters the café, into the smoke of war and the eyes of Abdul the Incorruptible, who signs to the two men.

Rantzau turns. The Satin Woman knows this tortured face from forgotten lives, or from some staircase in the dark where haunted men have passed without a flicker of desire for her ascending form. Yet his eyes almost speak as she approaches; but she is mistaken; he is one who moves down into the shadows, seeking a knight's catafalque, on which his cross is embroidered. There, she thinks, he will lie with the others before him, lips faintly smiling, as if his quest were won.

And it's only a fever, a dream of one stumbling in a foreign city. I know these ruined knights.

Nightingale speaks, introducing his old comrade, and Rantzau, trembling, rises for her.

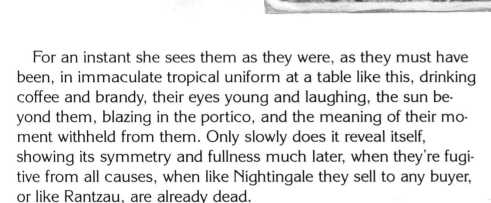

For an instant she sees them as they were, as they must have been, in immaculate tropical uniform at a table like this, drinking coffee and brandy, their eyes young and laughing, the sun beyond them, blazing in the portico, and the meaning of their moment withheld from them. Only slowly does it reveal itself, showing its symmetry and fullness much later, when they're fugitive from all causes, when like Nightingale they sell to any buyer, or like Rantzau, are already dead.

She sits, recognizing that now is but another photograph withholding its secret, that her stunning entrance is significant in ways that will always elude her, until the photograph is old as the Great War, and older. Then only will the disturbing veil of the present fall from it, and the effect she sought to create will finally appear, in gossamer rays to her ageing eyes.

Nightingale is looking at her; Rantzau has mumbled something. She feels the sun-streaked image forming, of this table and its flowered cups, and the flowered cloth as well. The rattan chairs, the awning, everything is arranged; here in the bright day a small party celebrated the meaning of life, with other strangers.

And none of us aware of what that meaning was. How unfair, she thinks, laying her bag by the leg of the chair where eternity would keep it.

Abdul the Incorruptible: Business is good. Soon I will have my own European ice machine.

Bagg stands before Gospodinoff. The servant has barely closed the door when Bagg begins to twitch. Light leaps from his eyes, his ears, and Gospodinoff draws backward, fearing he has given refuge to a saint.

The light ties itself into rings, divides into strands, spins up in balls, solidifies and crashes to the floor in a glittering heap.

Gospodinoff gapes at the jewels. More sparks shoot from Bagg's kneecaps and fingernails, and merge in a glowing mist which bursts, raining diamonds, rubies, emeralds. They clatter on the floor, a fine yellow powder clinging to their hard edges.

A last necklace drops from the end of Bagg's tongue. He accepts the cold drink offered by Gospodinoff, tries to sit down, finds a woman's small jeweled dagger in the seat of his pants. Wearily, he tosses it into the shining pile.

"I have seen nothing," says Gospodinoff, returning to his divan.

"Can you dispose of it?"

"The Arab chieftains."

"How long?"

"A week at the most."

"I have a boatman. Chinese. I'll send him round." Bagg gets to his feet. He feels immeasurably lighter. Gospodinoff does not try to detain him, shows him through the marbled hallways, to the front door.

"Should you need anything—a car, a companion, an obstruction removed from your path—don't hesitate to call me."

Bagg lumbers down the steps, crosses the courtyard, as Gospodinoff watches from the doorway. So, reflects the Greek, I have met the Gold Dust Bandit. Appearances are so often deceptive.

The main gate opens, and his clumsy disheveled guest passes through. Gospodinoff returns through the cool hall, to his study, where the treasure lies in a pile that is almost obscene.

It is a little-known fact of the desert that camels smoke. Their habit begins when the driver of the camel in front smokes his hubble-bubble and the smoke drifts backward, to the nose of the camel behind. Inhaling, the camel who follows comes to love the aroma. Soon he is marching along with a rolled cigarette wedged in his nostril, and smoke coming out from between his teeth.

In this way, the last hope of Major Medjid's company ever reaching its destination is lost. The Major is drinking hashish tea and continues to fight legendary battles on the walls of his tent. His map readers are flat out, tracing roads through the clouds. The camels used to know the way, but now they float along stupidly, enjoying scenery that isn't there, while Major Medjid and his second-in-command perform flanking maneuvers up the tent pole, against a monkey-headed enemy carrying knives in its tail.

Nightingale and the Satin Woman in the garden: He has his maps out, and his pistol, is enjoying new plans. A thin web floats down from the sycamore above him, and he brushes it away. It is followed by another, and another; snapping out of his daydream, he realizes he's being attacked. He leaps up, only to be tripped by a whirling cone of thread, glowing golden in the sunlight.

The cricket is startled in the marketplace by a rushing sound. Looking overhead, he sees his old brass cage descending. It hovers beside him, the lid opening like a crying mouth.

He hops inside and is quickly whirled away, over the crowded streets.

Nightingale struggles on the ground, but his arms are pinned by the weaving stuff. He sees the Satin Woman fall, entangled by the same golden net.

She tries to wriggle out, but the thread is electric, alive, anticipating her moves. The intimidating eye-spots on her wings are an empty threat, and she lies helpless in the sand, watching Nightingale crawl like a worm across the courtyard.

A limping step sounds in the near hall of the house. A pair of heavy boots appears at the doorway; a faint breeze brings her the smell of ginger.

The cricket's antennae are bent in the wind. His cage turns abruptly, makes a rapid descent. In a courtyard below, he sees glowing golden shapes, picks up their signal, and climbs to the edge of his cage.

The cage swoops in low; he leaps, onto the Satin Woman's shoulder, and the spinning thread closes him in beside her, in deep darkness.

The caterpillar lowers itself out of the sycamore trees, onto Bagg's sleeve.

"You're certain they won't be harmed in there?" Bagg stoops over the golden cocoons enclosing his prisoners. "Scotland Yard wants them alive."

"They'll be all right," says the caterpillar. "But why play policeman any longer? You have a fortune now. You are a sultan."

"It's a private matter," says Bagg, reflecting on the beat he's pounded, from Marrakech to Singapore, from Mandalay to Mozambique, across the months, and finally years, to take this pair, at last. A matter of pride. I don't expect a caterpillar to understand. "But after this case I retire."

"Good," replies the caterpillar. "And I shall find you a palace here in the sun, with jewel-encrusted towers."

"A small chalet in Switzerland will do, old man, if it's all the same to you."

The shoe cleaner, watching events in the broken bits of glass attached to his box, gives the command:

"Fly me to Cairo."

The box rises tentatively, wavers over the gutter.

"No hesitation. Allah has willed it."

The box moves along the curbstone, gradually gaining altitude. Then over the Golden Horn it flies, circling once, to chart a course. Istanbul is below, minarets gleaming. The shoe cleaner holds on to his hat.

"There is no God but God."

Abdul the Incorruptible enters Nightingale's courtyard by the back gate, the boatman behind him, pulling a veiled cart.

Bagg nods, the boatman closes the gate. Abdul looks down at the Satin Woman's enshrouded form and steps over it, toward Bagg. "All is proceeding satisfactorily?"

Bagg opens his wallet, counts out Abdul's fee. The boatman removes the veil from the cart, unloads two ancient coffins, pillaged from a tomb.

"The beauty of the Egyptian courtyard," says Abdul, "is that its activities are hidden from all."

He is unaware of the shoe cleaner, riding on his shoe box, upon the wind.

The cricket, alone with her in the suffocating blackness, speaks of stars and moons. They appear as he names them, in the depth of the night, and the Satin Woman lies comforted, as one who is merely resting on the sand, with the glittering bowl of heaven above.

"Love is a caravan," he whispers, *"winding forever."* And she sees its lamps appearing on the horizon, feels its age and mystery, watches the jinns of the sand fall enraptured as it approaches, its undulating shadows playing against the stars, its lamps beckoning to her, tongues swaying hypnotically.

The faces of the drivers are cloaked. Their number is great, and they sing of love's journey, of the worlds they have known.

One cloak slips from a darkened face, and Nightingale's camel kneels beside her in the dunes.

Rantzau lies feverish, teeth chattering, as the shoe cleaner flies through his window.

"Your comrade is in danger."

Rantzau stumbles from bed, staggers to the window. The shoe cleaner flies back out and hovers in the air on his twinkling box.

"But how am I to follow you?"

"Take anything," says the shoe cleaner. "Allah has willed it."

Rantzau looks at his bed roll, which lifts off the floor and glides timorously toward him.

"That's it," says the shoe cleaner. "Come on…"

Rantzau steps onto the floating roll and rides it out the window, following the shoe cleaner, over the rooftops of Cairo.

"Y̲ou have the papers?"

"But of course." Abdul the Incorruptible slips a hand into his shirt. "There were, unfortunately, some additional expenses encountered in procuring them…"

Bagg covers Abdul's palm once again, receives an official document in his own, granting him permission to remove, as part of an archaeological expedition, two sarcophagi from the country.

"You will have no trouble," the Incorruptible One explains. "Should you wish, you may take other items through as well. There are, as a matter of fact, twelve hundred sun helmets of unique design being offered at a special price to explorers…"

A flapping sound above them turns their heads. Rantzau drops down over the sycamore trees, draws his pistol, fires on Bagg. Gold dust pours from Bagg's wounds; he has only slight pain, but feels himself spilling, all his treasure going out from him. He knows jiujitsu, if he could just get a hold, but his opponent is floating around on a bedroll, just out of reach.

Ruined, thinks Bagg, for pride and 326 pounds a year, plus 5 pounds for boots. Just when fortune was in my hands.

Where is my caterpillar?

Abdul the Incorruptible slips out the front door, the golden worm in his palm.

"You must feed it four inches of flowered silk each day," says the boatman, slipping out beside him, into the street.

"It can be gotten at a discount," replies Abdul, "through an untarnished ship captain I know, who steals it direct from Hong Kong."

"Occasionally you must let it kill someone."

"Occasionally there are people who should be killed."

"You are more sensible than my previous employer."

"I have perfected my character through clean hands and decent feelings," answers Abdul, as they turn the corner, past the mosque of Mamluk Sultan El-Muayyad.

Bagg crawls in the courtyard, manages to rise, but the dust has all spilled from his arms and legs, and the old tunes are whirling in his brain. Coiners, sneak thieves, beggars, beware. Should there be a sudden death in the street, should the roadside subside, should a gas explosion occur, should he be assaulted, His Majesty's constable will act with decision and firmness…*oh…*

*there's a boy across the river
with a bottom like a peach…*

Alas, thinks Bagg, tumbling into Nightingale's fountain, I cannot swim. Bedroll and shoe box are still flying around him, and he realizes his mistake. A Lancashire lad shouldn't mix with the international set. Bishop's Gate police station is the place for him, unless he wants to get plowed. The man on the bedroll has plowed me, with, I believe, a *Mauser*.

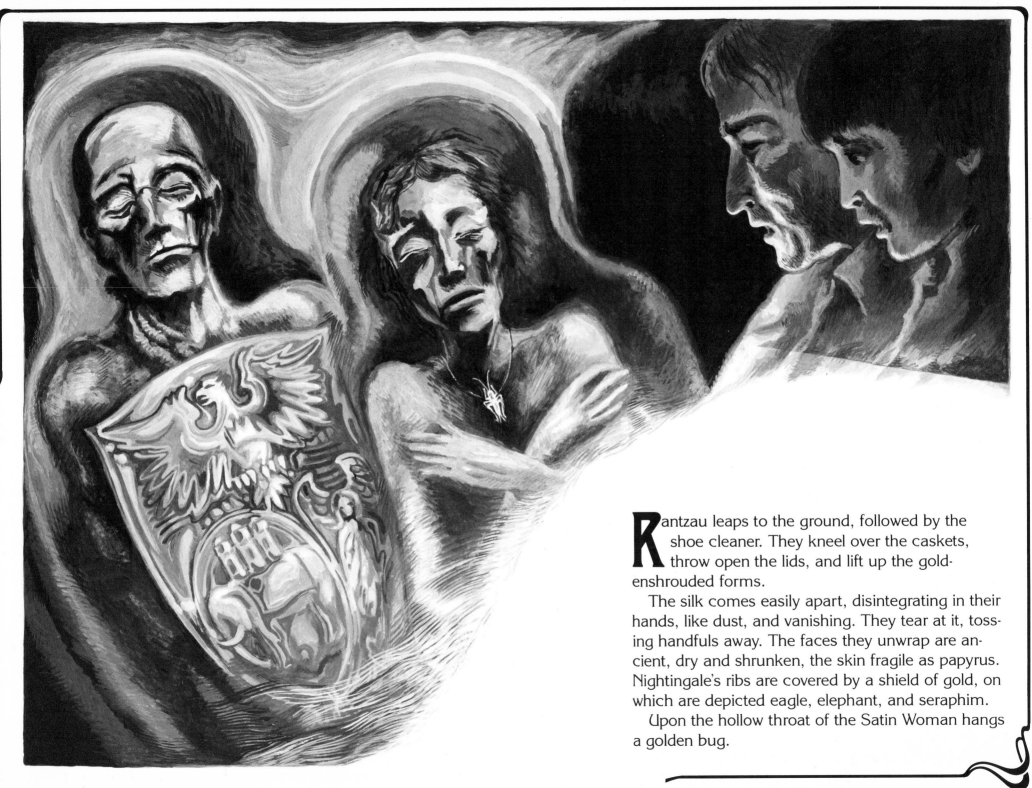

antzau leaps to the ground, followed by the
shoe cleaner. They kneel over the caskets,
throw open the lids, and lift up the gold-
enshrouded forms.

The silk comes easily apart, disintegrating in their
hands, like dust, and vanishing. They tear at it, toss-
ing handfuls away. The faces they unwrap are ancient, dry and shrunken, the skin fragile as papyrus.
Nightingale's ribs are covered by a shield of gold, on
which are depicted eagle, elephant, and seraphim.

Upon the hollow throat of the Satin Woman hangs
a golden bug.

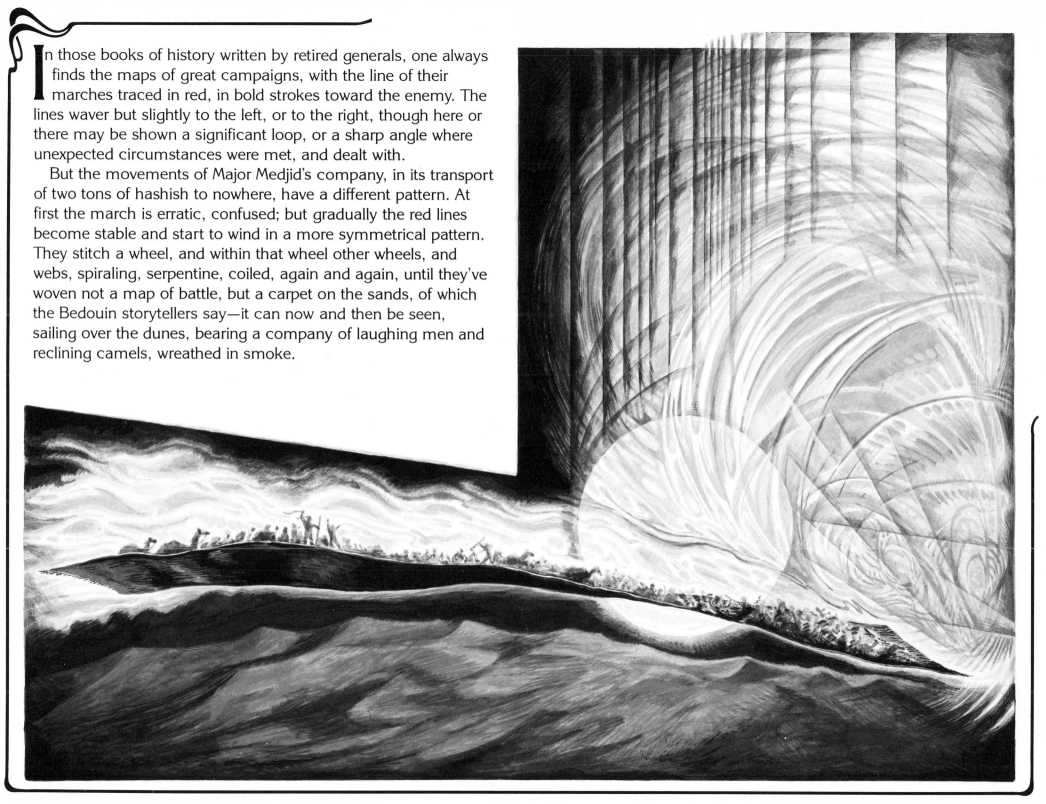

In those books of history written by retired generals, one always finds the maps of great campaigns, with the line of their marches traced in red, in bold strokes toward the enemy. The lines waver but slightly to the left, or to the right, though here or there may be shown a significant loop, or a sharp angle where unexpected circumstances were met, and dealt with.

But the movements of Major Medjid's company, in its transport of two tons of hashish to nowhere, have a different pattern. At first the march is erratic, confused; but gradually the red lines become stable and start to wind in a more symmetrical pattern. They stitch a wheel, and within that wheel other wheels, and webs, spiraling, serpentine, coiled, again and again, until they've woven not a map of battle, but a carpet on the sands, of which the Bedouin storytellers say—it can now and then be seen, sailing over the dunes, bearing a company of laughing men and reclining camels, wreathed in smoke.

And the caravan of love, whose route cannot be traced save in the heart of time, wanders on, its bells tinkling in the night, its number increased by yet another—who follows at a distance, accompanied by a pig.

Shortly thereafter, a clairvoyant in the Bishop's Gate district
receives a curious message she cannot interpret:

Following Nightingale. Trail quite hot.
Hope to collar him soon.

And Rantzau walks through Eastern streets, stopping at cafés and drinking quietly beneath their awnings. Always the old photograph is laid before him—of Nightingale and the others, smiling beside their cannon, on which they've placed two bottles of wine and some teacups. The sun in the photograph is brighter than the sun that blazes on the sidewalk beside him, and the faces in the photograph are alive—Nightingale so confident, and the wine half gone. Alive—Rantzau has only to look at them and they speak through the silence. *There is no death,* says the dog-eared yellowing talisman. *Our youth is preserved; in the sun of the desert we smile.*

He drinks again from the photograph, afraid sometimes he will drink it dry, yet new life always runs into it, and new mystery. When he dies in an alleyway off the marketplace, it and his Mauser prove to be his only possessions. The Mauser quickly disappears in the crowd; the photograph passes through so many hands it falls apart, and is discarded, the faces torn through, the eyes still smiling in the dust of the aged city.

The shoe cleaner, descending on his shoe box into Istanbul, hears the Satin Woman's footsteps everywhere—in the thoroughfares and all the little winding lanes.

He lands, takes up his trade again. In every shoe he works on she appears to him, veiled yet speaking softly with her eyes. Those customers who see her in the shine have good luck that day; those who don't, feel good anyway, their footsteps leading them to streets they've never seen before, where an unknown neighborhood quickens their soul, gates and windows revealing aspects of life they've previously known only in their dreams—everything shining with the sheen of satin, and greeting them intimately, like a woman desirous of love.

"Shine, sir? Shine, O illustrious potentate?"

119

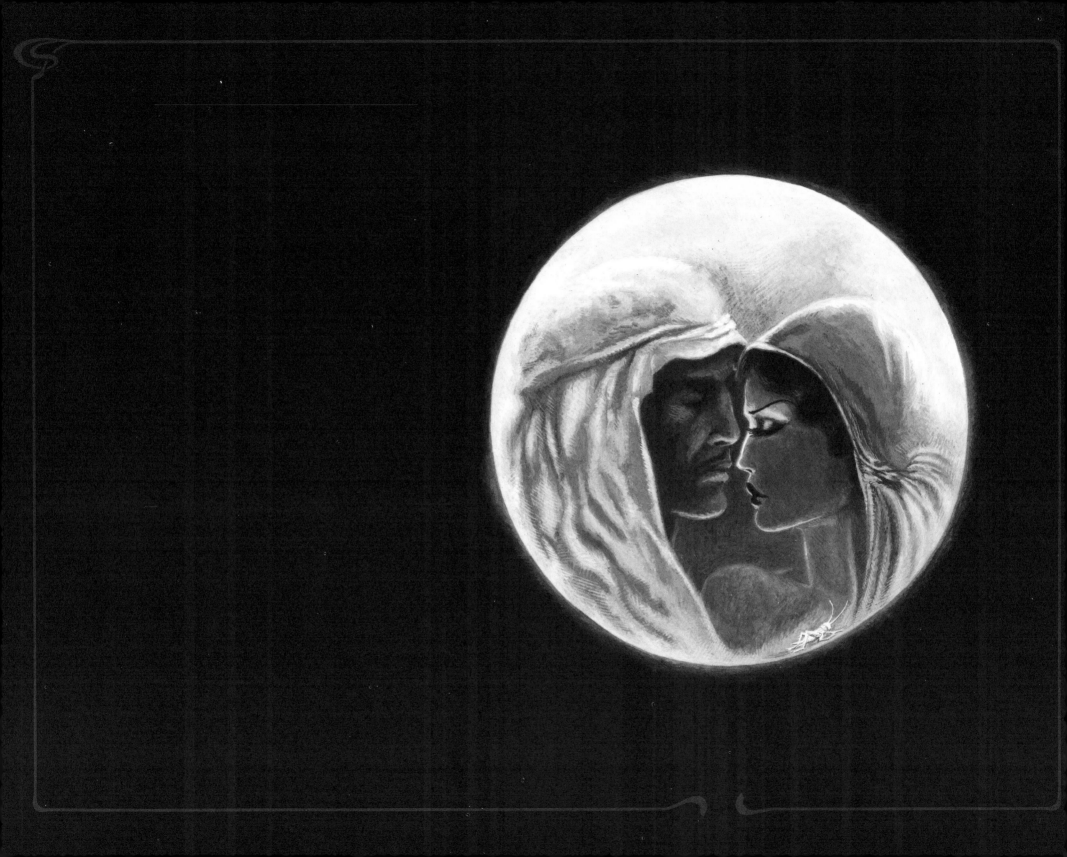